THE COLOR OF BLOOD

ALSO BY BRIAN MOORE

THE COLOR OF BLOOD

BRIAN MOORE

A William Abrahams Book

E. P. DUTTON · NEW YORK

Publisher's Note: This novel is a work of fiction.
Names, characters, places, and incidents either are
the product of the author's imagination or are used
fictitiously, and any resemblance to actual persons,
living or dead, events, or locales is entirely coincidental.

Published in the United States by E. P. Dutton,
a division of NAL Penguin Inc.,
2 Park Avenue, New York, N.Y. 10016.

Library of Congress Cataloging-in-Publication Data
Moore, Brian, 1921–
The color of blood.
"A William Abrahams book."
I. Title.
PR9199.3.M617C65   1987   813'.54   87-6695
ISBN 0-525-24539-1

OBE

Designed by Michele Aldin

10 9 8 7 6 5 4 3 2 1

First Edition

For Jean

1

The car taking him back to the Residence entered Proclamation Square sometime between nine and nine-fifteen. He had not looked at his watch since leaving the meeting. It was raining, a summer shower. In the square, the statues, roofs and monumental buildings were wetted slick; the pavement glistened. He switched on the pencil lamp over his clipboard to read, not his notes, but a small book by Bernard of Clairvaux.

Do you not think that a man born with reason yet not living according to his reason is, in a certain way, no better than the beasts themselves? For the beast who does not rule himself by reason has an excuse, since this gift is denied him by nature. But man has no excuse.

Sometimes, reading St. Bernard, he could abandon the world of his duties and withdraw into that silence where God waited and judged. But now he saw, peripherally, a black car racing very close to his. He turned to look. The driver, a woman, wore a green silk scarf tied around her head. Beside her in the passenger seat, a bearded man, holding a revolver in both hands, raised it, aiming at him. In that moment, Joseph, his chauffeur, wrenched the steering wheel around, deliberately crashing into the black car. Tumbled as in a centrifuge, he was buffeted and thrown clear, his body thudding on wet pavement. He lay for a long moment in a painful stupor staring at the ineluctable darkness of the night sky.

Car horns sounded: he heard running footsteps. Above him, looking down at him, was a young woman, a green silk scarf tied around her head, her face bleeding, pockmarked by tiny chips of glass. He raised himself to a sitting position and saw a large dark stain on her thigh where blood had oozed through her dress. "Are you all right?" he asked, foolishly. "Are you hurt?"

She did not answer. She turned and walked away, briskly, but with a limp, going in the direction of Market Street. Traffic, entering the square, slowed and stopped, mesmerized by disaster. He stood up and was dizzy. When his vision cleared he saw a middle-aged man staring at him from a car. "You . . ." the man said, as if searching for a name to call him. "Are you all right . . . Reverence?"

He nodded. He went toward the wreckage. Some men were trying to lift the black car clear of his old Mercedes. One of them, a policeman, called: "All together! One . . . two . . . go!" With an ugly sound the cars separated.

He looked at the wreckage underneath. He was used to death. It was part of his daily round. He knew the precise moment of its coming, the moment of the soul's departure. Joseph's body was broken, an arm loose in his chauffeur's jacket, a leg twisted, the foot turned backward. But Joseph's face was not injured. It was pale and composed as though a skilled surgeon had removed the intelligence behind it. Even as his mouth formed words of prayer, he knew that Joseph had been denied that which he would have most desired: the consolation of the last sacraments.

Police flares lit up in a staggered line across the square, casting an eerie orange glow as he turned from Joseph's body and walked to the other man. The man had been lifted from the wreckage of the black car and placed in a stream of headlights. Tiny bits of glass, jewel bright, glinted from his bearded cheeks and bleeding nose. As he bent down toward him he smelled a strong stench of vodka. "Can you hear me?" he asked, and the travestied face turned to look up at him. The eyes widened in anger or in fear, the mouth opened as though to speak. The dying face then turned away abruptly, as though dismissing him. But God's mercy is infinite. He knelt, made the sign of the cross and began the

———

3

prayer. As he did, some of the bystanders took off their hats as a mark of respect. While he prayed, two paramedics entered the stream of headlights, laid down a stretcher, then squatted, looking at the bearded man. "Drunk," one said. The other stood up and turned to the bystanders. "He's gone."

They lifted the body onto the stretcher and he looked again at the bruised, bearded face. Who is he? Why did he try to kill me? Joseph saved me. Joseph.

One of the paramedics came up and took hold of him, turning him toward the headlights, examining him as a mother examines a child. "How do you feel, Reverence? What hurts?"

"No, no," he said. "I'm all right. But there's another person injured. A woman."

"Woman?" The paramedic turned to the bystanders, searching. A man in a windbreaker stepped into the headlights' glare, a minor actor in the stage light, self-important in this, his moment. "There was only three involved," the man said. "The two dead ones and His Reverence."

"Eminence," a voice said from the darkness. "You call him Eminence. He's the Cardinal."

Who said that? Was it one of the "raincoats," the Security Police assigned to follow him? They, of course, must have seen the crash, the woman, everything. Where are they, the men in the blue Lada?

He turned to the darkness beyond the headlights. "Are any of you gentlemen here?" he asked.

No one answered. The paramedic who had examined him took him again by the arm. "You're dizzy, aren't you?" the paramedic said. "Come on. We'll take you in the ambulance."

In the ambulance they had placed Joseph's body in the lower rack. Now the stretcher squealed as they slid the bearded man's corpse onto the upper rack. He sat across the aisle from Joseph. Faces peered in at him as the paramedics pulled the door shut. The ambulance moved out, using its siren to clear the way, then shutting it off as it raced through empty, rain-wet streets. He prayed for the repose of Joseph's soul. Grant him eternal rest, O Lord, and let perpetual light shine upon him. Joseph, his hands rough as wood, lapping into folds the long crimson sash made in Rome, then carefully placing the crimson biretta on top. I, born a stableman's son, was instructed my first day as cardinal, by Joseph, a peasant from Kripke Province. "A cardinal must be seen by the people, Eminence. That's what the old cardinal said. And he said the red robes a cardinal wears are in memory of the blood Christ spilled for us. So wear them in honor, Eminence. Now let me help you with that sash." Joseph. Oh, Joseph.

The ambulance siren started up again, announcing their arrival as they drove into a courtyard. He knew this place: the former Holy Cross Hospital, now Marshal Konev Central District Hospital. The paramedics set up a portable wheelchair, then wheeled him in through swinging doors that were pulled open to receive him. In a bright-lit institutional hall, heavy with the reek of disinfectant, a cluster of medical personnel waited. Someone must have telephoned ahead to announce his coming. An older doctor in a white coat advanced, head bobbing respectfully, and would have kissed the episcopal ring had he not withdrawn his hand. They then wheeled him into a small examination room and made him sit on a high steel table. "If Your Eminence will please take off your jacket and shirt? The orderly will help you."

He did as he was told. The orderly slit open the end of his torn trousers, revealing that he had a cut running along the lower part of his leg. He asked if they would please telephone the Residence and tell Father Malik or Father Finder to come around with a car. A younger doctor, who was beginning to clean the cut on his lower leg, looked up and said it had already been done. He knew then that the raincoats had telephoned ahead. The older doctor examined his chest and put iodine and an adhesive bandage on an ugly-looking cut below his collarbone. Then a light shone in his eye: the doctor's eye, magnified, peered at him. "Just a slight concussion. Nothing more. You're exceptionally lucky, Your Eminence."

"It was a drunk driver, wasn't it?" the young doctor asked, glancing up at him.

"Was it?" He looked at the young doctor, but the doctor's face was innocent.

"Drink is the curse of this country," the old doctor said. "It's our national disgrace."

The old doctor then told the orderly to take him to X Ray. "Just to make sure." The orderly put a white gown on him and sat him again in the wheelchair. As they wheeled him down the corridor, he was followed by a stout woman carrying a clipboard. "Excuse me, sir," she said. "But we need some particulars. Your Christian name and surname."

"Bem," he said. "Stephen Bem."

"And how old are you?"

"Fifty-six."

"Place of birth?"

"I was born here. In the city."

As he spoke he saw Finder, his secretary for diocesan affairs, running up the corridor to meet him, fat, pale, alarmed. "How are you, Your Eminence?"

"I'm all right," he said. "But Joseph is dead. They brought his body here. Please find out what they're going to do with it."

They wheeled him into the X-ray room and made him lie on a cold steel slab. "Take a deep breath and hold it." He heard the whirr and click of machinery. "You can breathe out now." Drunk driver? The bearded man was drunk, perhaps, but he was not the driver. The driver was that young woman in the green scarf, the one who came up afterward to see if I was dead.

"We've finished, sir. You can get dressed now."

As he buttoned his shirt, a thin, nervous nurse came into the room. "Can we fetch you something, Your Eminence? A glass of tea?"

He saw by the crucifix on her uniform that she was a nun. "No, thank you, Sister."

"You wouldn't remember me, of course," she said. "The Sisters of the Holy Cross. But I spoke to you at our Jubilee celebrations last year."

"Yes," he said. "Yes, that was at Chernoya. Last spring."

Tears came to her eyes. "Thanks be to God, you were spared, Your Eminence. The country needs you."

Suddenly, she went to him, pulling at his hand, half curtsying as she kissed his ring. The technician coming out from behind the protective screen stopped and stared as though he had witnessed a pornographic act. "Too many people have cars today," the technician said, undoing his heavy lead apron and hanging it up. "People who're doing nothing for the country." He realized that with these words the technician was putting him on notice. The statement was a declaration of faith. The technician believed, not in God, but in the Party.

When they wheeled him out of the X-ray department Finder was waiting in the corridor with the older doctor. A good man, Finder, but alarmist. One could not confide in him or discuss certain matters as one could with Kris Malik.

"I have some sleeping pills for you," the older doctor said. "I've told Father Finder that you must be made to rest for the next few days."

"I never take sleeping pills, Doctor. And I have a great deal to do in the next few days."

"It's up to you, of course," the doctor said. "But you did have a nasty spill. It's a miracle that you escaped so lightly."

2

It was not a miracle, it was simply God's will, he thought as he got into the car with Finder. "What about Joseph?" he asked, as the car drove out into the broad expanse of New World Boulevard.

"They will release the body in the morning," Finder said. "It's just a formality."

He looked back. A blue Lada was following. "I

want Joseph's body brought to the cathedral. I will say a requiem mass. When can we fit it in?"

"Perhaps tomorrow morning, Eminence. You have no appointments between ten and twelve."

"Has anyone spoken to his wife?"

"No, I don't think so," Finder said. "When they telephoned, they didn't mention that the chauffeur had been hurt."

"Who was it who telephoned? Do you know?"

"They didn't say. Actually, they phoned the secretariat number. It was Father Krup who took the message."

The secretariat, the archdiocesan offices and the offices of the episcopal council were housed jointly in the archepiscopal residence on Lazienca Street. The building, a former princely palace, had, like the rest of the Old City, been razed by the Germans as an act of reprisal at the end of the Second World War, and subsequently rebuilt, stone by stone, in a gesture of national pride. This perfect restoration re-created the old palace with all its drawbacks, the dark corridors, the many useless reception rooms, the central court that reminded him of a prison exercise yard. By day, it was noisy and disorganized, its offices and hallways clamorous with petitioners, religious and civil. At night the gates were locked: all was silence. In the huge façade, brooding over Lazienca Street, isolated lighted windows shone like stars in a night sky.

But now, as the Residence gates were opened to admit them and they drove across the courtyard to the side entrance, all of the lights were on. Within the hall the secretariat priests, the Sisters of Nazareth, who did the housekeeping, the drivers, porters and yardmen were assembled to greet him. They crowded around solicitous and relieved, asking questions, offering assurances. But Finder announced in a loud voice that His Eminence was ill and must go straight to bed.

"Wait," he told Finder. "Is Teresa here?"

Joseph's wife came through the ranks. At once, seeing her face, he felt a coward's relief. She had already been told. He put his hand on her shoulder. The stuff of her gray servant's dress was rough to his touch as he led her into an anteroom at the far end of the entrance hall. He switched on the light and was at once face-to-face with a large statue of Jesus that stood just inside the door. The statue's hand, raised in the traditional gesture of blessing, seemed to caution him to be discreet.

He shut the door. "You have been told?"

She nodded. She had been weeping and her nose was red and wet. She wiped it, awkwardly, with the back of her hand. "Please," he said. "Won't you sit for a moment?"

"Oh, no, Your Eminence. It's yourself who should be sitting down."

"There will be a requiem mass for Joseph tomorrow morning in the cathedral. I will say the mass myself."

She bobbed her head. "Joseph will—I mean Joseph would be very honored, Your Eminence."

"He saved my life tonight."

She looked at him in surprise, then nodded. "Yes, he would," she said. She began to weep and once again he felt shame at not possessing that essential pastoral gift: the ability to comfort and console others in their time of grief. "I will be lost without him," he said, in desperation, staring at the plaster statue because he could not face her tears. The statue, hand upraised, seemed to take pity on him. Suddenly, he wept. And at last, seeing him weep, she forgot her awe of him.

"There now," she said. "There now. Oh, look at your coat, it's all muddy, Your Eminence. And your trousers. What would Joseph say if he saw you in that state? Now, don't you worry about me, sir. Go straight on up to your bed. And thank you, I mean thank you for the mass for Joseph."

His private quarters were on the fourth floor. Finder, who went up with him in the elevator, insisted on leaving the sleeping pills that the doctor had prescribed. Sister Agnes had placed a tray with his usual supper—cold meats, hot milk and oatmeal biscuits—beside the small single bed, which, in this large room, furnished otherwise in the style of a Middle European Grand Hotel, seemed as out of place as a servant's bed in a master's room. But he had brought this bed here, indeed had slept in it ever since his first days as a priest in faraway Gallin Province.

Now he sat on the bed unlacing his shoes, bending forward, presenting to the mirror in the wardrobe facing him the bald patch on his head of graying hair. As he straightened up he saw in the glass his torn trousers and stained clothes. I look like one of those poor drunkards who pass their nights sleeping under the arches of the Volya River. As he removed his jacket he felt for his watch. When he drew it out, the face was smashed, the hands missing. The watch had been a gift from his students at Wolna University. He doubted that it could be repaired. He put it in the drawer by his bedtable and took out a second pair of reading glasses to replace those he had lost in the accident. He stood up then and crossed the room in his stockinged feet looking for the pajamas and dressing gown that Joseph laid out each evening. As he did, someone knocked on the door of the study adjoining his bedroom.

"Is that you, Kris?"

His private secretary, Father Krystof Malik, tall, gray-haired, carrying a thick folder of papers, came in in his usual rushed, rumpled manner. "How are you, Eminence, are you all right?"

"I thought you were still in Gneisk, Kris."

"I came back on an early flight, Eminence. I wanted you to know the situation there."

"What *is* the situation?"

"Well, as I told you, I have a friend in the Archbishop's office in Gneisk. He's the one who called me. It seems he was asked to type a first draft of an address Archbishop Krasnoy plans to give at the Rywald celebrations next Tuesday. I have part of that sermon with me."

"And?"

"It's incredible. He seems to be asking for some sort of national demonstration against the government."

"At this time," he said. "He must be mad."

Again, he felt dizzy. He lowered his head and, for a moment, a small aura appeared in his left eye.

"Eminence, are you all right?" Malik asked.

"Yes, yes," he said.

"What happened tonight? Finder says it was a drunk driver."

"Not exactly. Someone tried to shoot me."

Malik dropped unceremoniously onto the worn leather sofa and stared dully at the toes of his shoes. "My God. Who?"

"There were two of them. A man and a woman. She was the driver."

"Do the police have them?"

"He's dead. I think the woman got away."

"Of course she got away, if *they* are behind it."

"If who is behind it, Kris?"

"The SP, Eminence."

"It doesn't make sense. Why would the Security Police want to kill me?"

Father Malik opened his cardboard folder and shuffled the many papers there. "Well, I know it sounds extreme, Eminence, but who knows what they might do if they thought you were trying to incite the people to revolt."

"What are you talking about?"

"Archbishop Krasnoy's address, Eminence. May I read you part of it?"

He nodded his consent. His back had begun to hurt and he felt his shoulder throb painfully where they had bandaged it. It was as though, until now, the shock of the accident had anesthetized him to his injuries. He saw Kris fumble with his reading glasses and hold up a scribbled sheet of paper. "The nation in this critical time is like a great forest at the end of a summer of dreadful drought. A spiritual and moral drought. On the floor of this forest are millions of pine needles. It takes only a spark to set them ablaze. And what is that spark? Is it not the recent proof that those who rule us hold the Church in the utmost contempt? This callous behavior toward the religious leadership of the nation could be the spark that will set the forest ablaze, a fire that will cleanse and purify. Much could be destroyed, but in the end the nation will be strengthened and preserved in its faith and its freedom. We must ask for God's help in our present plight. We must unite to show the strength of our national will. Here, in this place, on this day, at the shrine of the Blessed Martyrs, I call on all of you to stand behind the Church in this hour of need."

"Dreadful prose," he said.

"I'm afraid it's nothing to laugh about, Eminence."

"Did I say it was? What time is it? Let's try to reach Krasnoy on the telephone."

"Do you think that's wise, Eminence?"

"What I want to tell him is that there will be no such sermon given next Tuesday at Rywald—or anyplace else for that matter. And I don't care who's listening in. In fact, it's probably the quickest way of passing my message along to the government."

"True. But you know what Archbishop Krasnoy is like. What if he refuses to obey you?"

"I am the Primate. He may disagree with me but he will not openly defy me."

At that moment he heard a familiar scraping on the bedroom door. He went to the door and opened it. Bashar rushed in, big as a miniature pony, jumping up, pawing at him. "Down, boy," he said. "Down!" But he hugged the dog, burying his face in the heavy fur. What will Bashar do without Joseph? Joseph was his real master. "Poor boy," he said. "Poor boy."

He turned to Kris Malik. "Did I tell you Joseph saved my life tonight?"

"No."

"When he saw them aiming at me, he crashed into the other car." In the light of the flares, Joseph's face, white, composed, lifeless.

He stared at Kris Malik. "I will be lost without him," he said.

"Perhaps Tomas can take over as your driver and dresser," Malik said. "Will I ring the Archbishop, then?"

"Yes." He took hold of Bashar's collar and led him to where the oatmeal biscuits were. He fed one to the dog, patted his head, then settled him down on his usual blanket at the foot of the narrow single bed.

"Your Eminence?"

"Yes, Kris?"

"I have the Archbishop on the line."

He took the receiver, noting with displeasure the complicit smile on Kris Malik's face. It is my fault, that smile. I should not have made fun of Krasnoy's prose. When will I learn to be a leader? "Yes," he said. "Is that you, Henry?"

"Stephen." Krasnoy's voice, loud and arrogant, at once brought to mind a picture of the man: the florid features, the pouting full lower lip. "How are you? Are you all right?"

"I am not all right. I have just read what is supposed to be part of an address you are planning to give next week at the Rywald celebrations—"

"How did *you* get hold of my address?"

"Never mind. What are you trying to do, Henry, start a bloodbath?"

"I wrote it as a warning, Stephen, purely as a warning."

"A warning to whom?"

"To General Urban. Who else!"

"I see. Has Rome made a special announcement appointing you as cardinal primate of this country?"

"I am sorry, Stephen. But many of the bishops and most of the lower clergy feel as I do. We cannot turn our backs on the people at this point in time."

"You are turning your back on *me*, Henry."

"Stephen, I would hope that is not true."

"Then let's make sure it is not true. Your address at Rywald will recall the faith of the September Martyrs. It must be an address about God, not politics. Rywald is a place of pilgrimage, not a rallying ground for political action. Is that understood, Henry?"

He could hear Krasnoy's breathing in the silence that followed. "I said, is it understood, Henry? Henry, are you there?"

He waited. At last, the words. "Yes, Eminence. Understood." In faraway Gneisk, the receiver clicked down. He turned to Father Malik's too-gleeful smile.

"Short," Kris Malik said. "And to the point."

"Good night, Kris," he said, and noted surprise and a slight unease on his secretary's face.

"I'm sorry, Eminence. You must be exhausted."

"Yes, I'm tired," he said. "And I don't think we should mention this to anyone. Also, in the matter of Joseph's death, I haven't said that someone tried to shoot me. I don't think it advisable under the present circumstances. I didn't even tell Joseph's wife. All right?"

"Yes, of course, Eminence. Very wise. Well, good night, Eminence. I hope you sleep well. I'll see you in the morning."

"Good night, Kris."

The door shut. In the silence of the bedroom he turned to the fireplace. There on the mantelpiece sat an old sepia tint of his father, so familiar that he had not looked at it for years. But now, surprisingly, the photograph seemed to come alive. His father stared out at him, eyes filled with anger and alarm, as though there were some danger in the room. He went to the photograph and picked it up. His father, his face disfigured by the heavy mustaches of pre-war days, stood in front of a row of horse stalls, in the main walk of Prince Rostropov's stud farm on the outskirts of the city. He wore riding breeches and a new tweed jacket and carried a riding crop, symbol of his elevation from head stableman to trainer of the Prince's racehorses. And in that instant, looking at the photograph, there came to mind the bruised, bearded face of tonight's assailant. It was, like his father's, a face that belonged in the past, the face of a member of the minor nobility, landed gentry, a man his father would have greeted by a deferential touch of his fingertips to the peak of his riding cap. Could it be possible? He replaced the photograph on the mantelpiece. Anything is possible now. He turned to the large uncurtained windows that looked out, not to the interior court, but on Lazienca Street itself. There, parked in its usual place, a block away from the gates of the Residence, was the inevitable blue Lada. The night shift was easy for the raincoats: he rarely went out after dark. He had often wondered if they took turns sleeping, or if both simply curled up and went to sleep in the car, shortly after he had switched off his bedside lamp. Now he looked beyond the street to the night lights of the city, flickering in a gimcrack maze. In the dead center of those lights a fat, winding arm of total blackness: the Volya River. He thought of the River Styx: the grim boatman. He thought of Joseph.

At the far end of the room was a small prie-dieu. A red votive candle burned there under a lithograph of the bruised Christ-face found on the Turin shroud. He knelt at the prie-dieu and bowed his head.

Examination of conscience. I lack all charity. Tonight, I was arrogant in my dealings with Henry Krasnoy. Also, I allowed myself to enter into collusion with Father Malik by my spiteful, malicious remark. I led him to mock one of Your archbishops. And Joseph? Did I accept Your will? Should I not rejoice that Joseph has gone to join You? Also, I should remember that two men, not one, died tonight because of me. That man who tried to kill me: grant him peace, O Lord.

I am Your servant, created by You. All that I have I have through You and from You. Nothing is my own. I must do everything for You and only for You. Tonight at the meeting I was obsessed by politics. I thought of the danger to our nation. I did not think of the sufferings we cause You by our actions. My fault, my most grievous fault.

3

A knocking, hurried, almost surreptitious, shocked him from prayer. "Your Eminence?" a voice whispered. It was not a voice he recognized. He rose and went to the study door. "Yes?"

"It's Bujak."

He opened at once. Bujak, the night porter, flustered, bobbing his head. "Father Finder sent me, Your Eminence. The Security Police. They're downstairs."

"At this time of night? What do they want?"

"They're coming up, Your Eminence. Will you see them?"

But as the porter spoke, he saw men at the top of the stairs: three raincoats, and, behind them, Finder, protesting. "I told you His Eminence is asleep. You have no right to come in here."

But they had seen him. They came on purposefully. Behind in the bedroom he heard Bashar growl. The one in the lead wore a summer straw hat of a cocoa brown color that made him look like an American tourist. But his face was the face of a member of the *nomenclatura:* those who considered him, his church, his position, an affront to their power.

"Cardinal Bem?"

"I am Bem."

The man held out a plastic-covered photograph of himself. Underneath it, the legend MAJOR. INTERNAL SECURITY POLICE. Usually, they did not bother to show identification. So it must be serious.

"Why were the gates locked?" the man asked.

"Because it is after eight. We close our gates at eight."

"The gates should not be locked against the representatives of the people."

"Indeed," he said. "And do you not lock your door when you go home at night, Major?"

"Your people did not admit us. They tried to keep us out."

"I am sorry about that," he said. "What can I do for you?"

"I have instructions that you are to come with us at once. You may pack a small suitcase. Are these your quarters?"

"Yes. But just a moment. I am to come with you where? If you will please wait, I am going to telephone the Minister for Religious Affairs."

At once he saw anger, or was it fear, in the man's eyes. "I have instructions that you are to telephone no one."

He looked past the first man and saw that one of the other raincoats had, surreptitiously, slipped a revolver from his pocket. He pointed to the gun. "What does this mean?"

"Come on, sir," said the one in the brown straw hat. "I am asking you politely. Put some clothes and toilet articles in a bag. Just enough for a few days. But hurry."

"We will protest," Finder said. "We will protest this at the highest level."

The one in the brown hat beckoned. "This way please, sir."

One of the other raincoats stayed behind in the corridor and the third, the one with the gun, went ahead into the bedroom as though to make sure no one was hiding inside. Bashar growled and there was a scuffling sound. "Shit!" the man cried. "Get him off me!"

He ran into the bedroom. To his surprise Bashar had cornered the man and stood, hackles up, showing his teeth. "Bashar!" he said, surprised. "No, no, don't worry. He won't bite you. He's harmless."

"Is he?" the Security man said. He held out his hand. It was bleeding. "You're lucky I didn't shoot him."

"I'm terribly sorry," he said. "Wait." He hurried toward his bathroom, the one in the brown hat following behind him.

"What are you doing?" the brown hat called. "Hold on there, sir."

But he ignored this. He opened the medicine cabinet, took out iodine and a bandage, then turned and went back into the bedroom calling: "Bashar! Down!" Bashar, contrite, tail-wagging, went to his blanket. He took the injured Security Policeman by the arm and led him to the bathroom sink. "Come along. Let's clean that up. I'm really very sorry about this." He ran water in the sink and put the man's bleeding hand under it.

"We haven't got time," the Security Major said.

"Of course you have time," he said. He dried the man's hand and sat him on the edge of the bathtub. He then knelt in front of the man and uncorked the disinfectant. "Bashar doesn't have rabies," he said. "But I think you should get an antitetanus shot, all the same."

The Major turned and went out of the bathroom. "Where is your suitcase?" the Major called. And then: "Bring that other priest in and tell him to pack for the Cardinal."

When he applied the iodine the policeman winced. "I'm sorry. That must hurt," he said. "But the bite isn't deep. Hold still."

He heard Finder call out. "Your Eminence, do you want me to pack for you? What shall I pack?"

"Hold on," he said. "I don't know why everyone's in such a hurry." He finished bandaging the policeman's hand, then got up off his knees and went back into his bedroom. "A few days, you said? Where are you taking me? To prison?"

"No, no," the Security Major said. He had gone to the window to look out. Now he turned back and there was sweat on his face. It was a hot August night but the sweat was excessive.

"Father Finder, get me the Minister's office."

"The Minister's office is closed," the Security Major said. "Besides, I told you, I have instructions that you are to telephone no one."

"May I ask why?"

"Please, sir, will you please start packing?"

He went to his wardrobe to look for shirts. His cassocks were hanging there. Hardly suitable wear for pacing a cell. He caught a glimpse of himself in the triptych mirror, saw his trousers, ripped to the knee. "I have to change," he told the Security Major.

"Yes, yes, go ahead."

They watched as he stripped to his underwear and took down a clerical summer suit. He put it on and pulled a sock painfully over his bandaged lower leg. He sat down, tied his shoes and, as he finished, looked up at the Security Major. "May I ask where you are taking me?"

"We are taking you into protective custody," the Major said. "We have been told to request your cooperation and the cooperation of your staff. No one must know that you have left these premises. Those are my instructions, sir."

"Why?"

"Because that was not an accident tonight. Are you aware of that?"

"I am."

"Excuse me, Eminence," Finder said. "But did I miss something? The police said it was a drunk driver. This is just some trick of these gentlemen, I'm sure."

He ignored Finder. He took a small suitcase from the bottom of his wardrobe and put some shirts in it. He opened a drawer, looking for socks and underwear. "I will need my breviary," he said. "Father, would you bring it? It's on my desk."

"Hurry, please," the Security Major said. He took off his brown straw hat and began to wipe sweat from the inner headband.

"You have not answered my question," he told the Security Major. "What do you mean, 'protective custody'?"

The Security Major shrugged. "That is what we call it."

He turned and went into the bathroom for his toilet case. "How is your hand?" he asked the other policeman. The policeman did not answer. When he put his toilet articles in the suitcase, the Security Major at once shut the suitcase and picked it up.

"All right, let's go."

"Your breviary, Eminence," Finder said, handing it to him. "Shall I telephone the Papal Nuncio?"

"I think not," he said. "Besides, I believe Monsignor Danesi is on vacation. He's probably in Italy now."

"I told you," the Security Major said. "You are to telephone no one."

As they came downstairs, two of the Sisters of

23

Nazareth were waiting in the hall with Bujak, the night porter. "Where is Father Malik?" he asked.

"I don't know, Your Eminence," one of the nuns said. "I think he went out after supper."

By the hall door he saw a fourth raincoat. This raincoat nodded to the Security Major. "Ready, sir."

They led him through the kitchens, going toward the service entrance at the rear of the building. The entrance gave, not on Lazienca Street but on a small side street called Mokotowa. Two cars were waiting in this street. Finder, hurrying alongside, said in Latin, "I will get in touch with Bishop Wior and I will also inform the Nuncio's office."

He answered in Latin. "I don't want to worry Rome with this, just yet. First try to find out where they are taking me."

"Stop it," the Security Major said. "Is that Latin? It *is* Latin, isn't it? I went to the Benedictine school."

They were now at the service-entrance door. The Security men blocked the entrance, preventing the nuns and Finder from following him outside. In each of the waiting cars was a plainclothes driver. The cars were not the normal blue Ladas, but an old station wagon and a red Volvo. He supposed these were spy cars, used by the police for covert surveillance. The Security Major led him to the red Volvo and put him in the backseat. The driver of the Volvo was smearing the back windows with a greasy substance that made it impossible to see in or out. The Security Major got in the front seat and the other SP men ran across the street and climbed into the old station wagon, which then pulled out ahead of the Volvo. The cars did not turn right into Lazienca

Street but drove down Mokotowa and through several back streets until they reached the Old Plaza. "Which prison is it?" he asked the Security Major. "Surely not the Citadel?"

"You are not going to prison," the Major said. "You will be comfortable. We are not your enemy, sir. We are taking you out of the city for a few days. Purely for your own protection."

"Who was the man who tried to kill me?"

The Security Major did not answer.

4

It was not a hotel. It was not a prison. When they brought him in from the car, he saw only a long hallway, a flight of uncarpeted stairs, a corridor and the room. The room contained a single bed, two shabby plush-covered armchairs, a pine table and a pine writing desk. Over the blocked-up fireplace was a set of stag's antlers. The windows were shuttered. When they left him alone he at once opened the shutters. All was darkness outside. He lay down but did not sleep. After many hours he saw gray light filter across the floor. He rose, feeling his shoulder throb with pain, and went again to the shutters. Opened, they revealed a yard enclosed by a high stone wall. In the yard several chickens fretted about amid a spill of newly scattered seed. The chickens, pecking dementedly, darted this way and that with worried, nervous looks. Irrationally, he thought: They too are prisoners in this place.

At the far end of the yard he saw a rusting tractor. On the other side of the stone wall was a plowed field. There were no other buildings on the horizon. A man came walking down the plowed field. He wore a green loden coat and a hunter's hat and held a rifle at the ready as though at any moment he might raise it and blow some small animal to pieces. But the man was not a hunter. At the other end of the field a second man appeared, also in a loden coat and carrying a rifle. The second man waved to the first man, then walked off out of sight. They were Security Police. The chickens, the tractor, the building, which looked like the country estate of some member of the prewar nobility, were disguises to deflect the attention of passersby. This place was, in all probability, one of those secret houses to which the regime brought people, once important, who then suddenly disappeared from view.

He felt for his watch and remembered that it had been broken. Normally, he rose at six-thirty to say mass in the residence chapel. Today he would have deferred his mass in order to officiate at the cathedral requiem for Joseph. *Joseph.* I hope Finder remembers to arrange it. But will anyone remember anything, after last night? What will the bishops do about my disappearance? Will they try to make public the fact that I have been arrested? I hope not. That could start the "fire" that Krasnoy prays for.

He looked out across the empty field. The sun rose in the sky behind a gauzy morning mist. It will be a hot day, one of those summer days when the city's squares and streets are close and clammy, when tempers grow short and people sit on their balconies in a state of half undress, drinking cold tea and complaining that there is nowhere to go to find relief from the heat. Days when the city's churches are empty, dark, cool and peaceful. But no one thinks to go there.

He turned from the window and, bowing his head, began his morning prayers. After several minutes he heard footsteps in the corridor outside. He turned toward the sound and noticed, for the first time, that there was a washbasin in his room and that they had left him soap and a towel. He found his toilet case and began to shave. As he turned the water faucet on, he heard someone cough in the room next to his. The person who coughed then walked across the floor and turned on a water faucet. So the wall must be thin. He went to it, knocked tentatively and waited.

His knock was returned.

"Hello," he said, raising his voice.

"Speak quietly," said a man on the other side of the wall. "Who are you?"

"A priest."

"You are? I also. I am Father Prisbek. What is your name?"

"Bem."

"*Cardinal* Bem?"

"Yes."

"So, it's true," said the voice through the wall. "They brought you here last night?"

"Yes. How long have *you* been here?"

"They're coming," said the voice. A moment later he again heard footsteps in the corridor. The footsteps stopped at the room next to his and he heard mumbled voices, the sound of a door opening, then footsteps retreating. He went again to the wall and knocked.

"Are you there?"

There was no answer.

Far away he heard shouts, as though someone issued orders. Then again, footsteps. This time they came directly to his door. A key turned in the lock.

This morning the Security Major wore a brown woolen cardigan and green corduroy trousers. He carried a tray on which were a glass of tea, a spoon, a roll with butter and two little jars, one containing honey, the other sugar. "Good morning, sir," the Major said, entering and putting the tray down on the table. "We didn't know if you took honey or sugar in your tea. So I brought both."

"Thank you," he said. The Major smiled in an ingratiating manner and walked back to the door. "I'll return shortly, sir."

"Wait. I would like to speak to someone in authority. And at once."

"Of course," the Major said.

"It's urgent."

"Yes," the Major said. "Yes."

The door shut. He noted that the Major had not relocked it. When the footsteps retreated he picked up the glass of hot tea and went back to the window. Below, in the yard, two persons were walking to and fro, conversing in low urgent tones. One was a priest, a tall young man with a wispy red beard. The other was a middle-aged woman who wore a short white headdress and a blue habit. He did not recognize her order. He looked for the raincoats who must be guarding them. But there were no raincoats in the yard. He looked over the wall to the field where he had seen the two SP men disguised as hunters, patrolling. But the SP men were nowhere in sight. Suddenly, unthinkingly, he called down to the yard. "Hello there! Hello?"

The nun stopped talking and looked up at him. She then turned as if for guidance to the young priest, who at once made a small furtive gesture as though to discourage her from answering. With a nod for her to follow, the young priest walked away from the window. He watched the nun as she ran to catch up. Both disappeared around a corner.

What sort of prison is this? There have been no reports of priests being arrested in the past few months. The Minister for Religious Affairs assured me that even the most right-wing priests have all been freed. Or has there been some new wave of arrests in the past twenty-four hours?

He turned away from the window and remembered that the Major had forgotten to lock the door. He put down his glass of tea, opened the door and went out into the corridor. The room next to his was now empty, the door ajar. He looked in. There was a washbasin and a bed bereft of pillow or blankets. He walked on down the corridor. From the silence he sensed that there were no other prisoners on this floor. At the end of the corridor was the flight of uncarpeted stairs he remembered from last night. He went down. On the wall in the hall he read a printed notice, faded with age.

OSTROF DISTRICT
SCHOOL OF ANIMAL HUSBANDRY

INSTRUCTION: JAN. 4–MAY 30
SEPT. 1–DEC. 23

To the left of the hallway was a large institutional dining room. It was empty. There were pickle jars and used dishes on the wooden tables. To the right of the hallway he saw a room with green blackboards, school desks and a lectern. It also was empty. Far away at the other end of the building he heard a faint sound that gradually became the footsteps of someone approaching. The green baize door at the rear of the hallway banged open and the Security Major came into view. He smiled. "Well," he said. "Found your way downstairs, I see. Sorry I didn't get back to you. But everyone's at a meeting."

"Who is everyone? Where is this place?"

"Oh, the place isn't important," the Security Major said. "But I have good news for you. The gentleman you wish to see is available now. If you'll come this way, please?"

They went through the green baize door and were in a rear corridor that, he surmised, led to the kitchens. Off this corridor was a small room, a sort of office, with agricultural-school notices tacked to a cork notice board and a large rolltop desk littered with overflowing correspondence trays. At the desk a man sat, writing. He looked up. He indicated a chair facing the desk. The Security Major smiled and withdrew, closing the door.

The man at the desk wore the sort of gray sharkskin suit that seemed to be the unofficial uniform of SP men of higher rank. Sparse blond hair rose like an aureole from the back of his neck. His skin was pink and clean as though he had just come from a steam bath and he smoked a long Russian cigarette, half cardboard filter, half tobacco. Now he exhaled smoke, smiling behind it as though it were a mask. "I am Colonel Poulnikov," he said. "Internal Security. I believe you wanted to see me?"

"I would like to speak to the Minister for Religious Affairs. At once."

"I am authorized to speak for the Minister."

He looked at the man. There was no sign of hostility in Colonel Poulnikov's face. In the past when he had spoken with senior raincoats the atmosphere had always been one of excessive civility on both sides. Of course, nothing of this sort had occurred before.

"Tell me, Colonel. Is it your intention to insult me?"

"I don't understand."

"I am the Cardinal Primate of this country, the head of the Church. In the past I have always been addressed by title, or as 'Eminence,' by the Minister, by your colleagues and, indeed, by the Prime Minister himself."

The man's pink skin reddened to a blush, which made him seem younger than before. "I beg your pardon, Eminence," Colonel Poulnikov said. "I was remiss. Please accept my apologies. I'm afraid I have had no experience in dealing with cardinals."

"All right, we will let it pass. Now, will you please tell me why I have been arrested and brought here? And what is this place?"

"It's an agricultural college, Your Eminence. It's not in use at the moment—the summer break, you know. So we have taken it over as your temporary residence. You have not been arrested, Your Eminence. You have been taken into protective custody, just for a week or so. We have arranged for a priest to act as your chaplain, assistant or whatever

---

you call it. As I said, I am not conversant with clerical terms. And we have a nun, Sister Martha, who will act as your housekeeper. We very much hope that your stay with us will be pleasant and without incident." He picked up a box of cigarettes lettered in the Cyrillic alphabet. "Do you smoke, Your Eminence?"

"Are you a Russian?"

Again, the Colonel seemed to blush. "Well, I'm surprised to hear you ask that, Your Eminence. I think your mother came from Kripke Province. So did mine."

"I'm sorry," he said. "Forgive me, I had no right to be rude. I suppose I am a little confused this morning. Will you be good enough to tell me the government's reason for this 'protective custody'?"

"Yes," the Colonel said. "Yes, of course. Someone—we suspect a fanatic of some rightist group—we have not yet identified the dead man correctly as he carried false papers—but, as I said, someone tried to kill you last night. And we have reason to believe that your life is still at risk. Now, it is the opinion of the Minister that if such an attempt were to succeed, it would cause great civil unrest and endanger the State in ways which . . ." The Colonel did not finish the sentence but, instead, drew on his cigarette and expelled smoke in a burst as though he were miming an explosion. "So we feel that, until we track down this terrorist group, it is better that your whereabouts be unknown, even to the Church authorities."

"Why, may I ask?"

"Because we have reason to believe, Your Eminence, that this group may be connected with reactionary elements within the Church itself."

"You mean that these people who are trying to kill me are Catholics?"

"In the opinion of the Minister, Your Eminence, that is more than a supposition. It is a fact."

"Ridiculous."

"Is it?" Colonel Poulnikov's pink cheeks flushed again as though something had shocked him. His voice rose to an edge of anger. "To them, you are the prelate who has betrayed your church, the cardinal who has sold out to the Communists. You have rendered unto Caesar the things that are God's."

He stared at the man. "Is that what they say about me?"

The Colonel, curiously sheepish, nodded and laughed. "Yes, Your Eminence. Yes."

"And they would kill me?"

"Some of them, yes. The lunatic fringe, I suppose."

In the small cluttered office, the silence that followed was broken by the bumbling of a large housefly against the windowpane. The morning sun, summer hot, spilled across the overflowing correspondence trays on the Colonel's desk. There is authority in what he says: he bathes daily in a running tap of words inspired by fear and greed, in secret reports of unwary talk, in denunciations inspired by hatred, words spoken after torture. It is the State's business to know these things. The Church has no comparable intelligence.

"You say you do not know who these people are?"

"No, sir, not yet. But it is our hope that if you remain here as our guest for a few days, we will be able to discover and arrest those who are responsible."

33

"I must speak to the Minister now."

"I am afraid that is not possible, Your Eminence."

"It must be possible! Are you aware—of course you are—that next Tuesday is the Jubilee celebration at Rywald? I must attend those ceremonies. Tell the Minister that if I am not allowed to attend the celebration he *will* have trouble on his hands."

"What sort of trouble, Your Eminence?"

"I do not wish to discuss it with you."

The Colonel rose and made a small old-fashioned bow. "I will speak to my superiors as soon as possible. Have you had breakfast?"

"Yes."

"Perhaps you would like to go for a walk now? It's a nice morning."

"A walk?" he said. "Where? In the prison yard?"

The Colonel smiled. "No, no, this is not a prison, Eminence." He went to the door, opening it. In the corridor outside, the red-bearded priest sat on a rush-bottomed chair reading his breviary. "Father Prisbek?"

The priest stood up. "Yes."

"His Eminence would like to go for a walk."

The Colonel turned, smiling, and again made his little bow. "I'll contact you very shortly, Your Eminence."

The bearded priest nodded, signaling to him to follow as though they were about to start on a duty tour of some school or orphanage. He followed the priest along the corridor and through the green baize door into the front hall. In the hall, the stout middle-aged nun sat on a bench, her hands in her lap. She looked at him shyly, then rose, bobbing her head in a gesture of respect.

———

"This is Sister Martha," the bearded priest said. Again, she bobbed her head. "And I am Father Prisbek." He lowered his voice to a whisper. "We spoke already. Through the wall."

"Are we going outside?" the nun asked, and looked around in the furtive manner of a prisoner. But there was no one in the hall. Prisbek opened the heavy front door and they all three went outside.

In addition to the chickens in the yard there were four Friesian cows in stalls and, near the rusting tractor, someone had piled several heavy bags of fertilizer. They went toward a gate that Prisbek opened by raising a heavy iron bar from a slot across the center. Outside, they stepped carefully, avoiding a pool of cow dung where cows had clustered, waiting to be brought in.

"This way, Your Eminence," Prisbek said. He pointed to a wooded area ahead. "It's quiet down there. It's a nice place for a walk." The nun, again with a furtive look around, came up beside him as they started along the path that led to the wood.

"We were sorry to hear about your chauffeur," she said. "Innocent people, Your Eminence, they're the ones who suffer."

"Who told you about my chauffeur?"

Again, she looked about in her furtive way, although to his surprise there seemed to be no guard in sight. "The raincoats. They told us this morning."

"How long have you been here then, Sister?"

"Three days, Your Eminence."

"And you?" He turned to Prisbek, who walked one pace behind.

"Three days also, Eminence. We were both brought here on the same day."

"Why?"

Prisbek shrugged. "I don't know. They told us you were coming to stay and that we must help make your stay as comfortable as possible."

"Yet the accident happened only last night," he said, stopping to look at both of them. But they moved on as though he had not spoken. At last, the nun said in her whispery voice, "I think they brought us here because they want to please you, Your Eminence."

"What are you talking about? Why should the government want to please me?"

"Because they respect you, Your Eminence. They know you're helping as much as you can."

He glanced at her surreptitiously as they walked on. She had a large hairy mole on her cheek. There was something about her half-furtive manner that disturbed him and, reviewing what she had said, he decided that she was not a prisoner here. She and Prisbek were probably members of the Organization of Patriotic Clergy, that group of Catholic religious formed by Father Bialy, sponsored by the government because they had accepted the aims and edicts of the Party. That is why there are no guards with us. These are my guards.

He turned and looked at the bearded priest. "What is your parish, Father Prisbek?"

"I am not in parish work."

"Where are you stationed, then?"

He saw the man hesitate. Perhaps he was not a priest at all. Then Prisbek said, "I am a teacher of mathematics at Majanow Seminary."

A lie. Majanow was in Bishop Bednortz's diocese and anything but a hotbed of the Patriotic

Clergy. Still, they had probably coached this man in his role. "Where are the guards?" he asked, in Latin.

"They are watching us from the wall," Prisbek answered at once.

So he is a priest. "And what did the raincoats say your duties are, Father Prisbek?"

"I am to act as your chaplain. I have arranged that you will be able to say mass here."

"And you, Sister?"

"They told me Your Eminence has stomach ulcers and that you will require a special diet. I am to supervise your meals."

"They are out of date."

"I beg your pardon, Eminence?"

"I no longer have a special diet. Anyway, it's irrelevant. I shall be leaving here as soon as I speak to the Minister for Religious Affairs."

He saw them exchange glances. "Is the Minister a friend of yours, Eminence?" the nun asked.

"Of course not."

"But he's not an enemy," the nun said with her strange smile. "I mean you don't *think* of him as an enemy, do you, Eminence?"

"I don't think of anyone as my enemy," he said. "Nor should you, Sister."

They had reached the wood. Ahead, between the trees, he saw a well-traveled path leading to a small glade where there was a picnic table and wooden benches. As they walked up the path, suddenly there was a deafening sound overhead. Like a shadow of death, a blur of blackness shut out the sun. Then the black shape materialized as a great silver cigar of jetliner, flying low over the trees as though on an approach path to a landing. Staring up

---

37

he saw, briefly, the wing markings and identified them as LOT, the insignia of the Polish airline that flew into the capital twice weekly. A plane on an international flight, passing over this low, must mean that we are not far from the city. As the noise subsided he looked at Prisbek, a question on his lips, a question he decided not to ask. Prisbek would lie. Prisbek and the nun may have been put here to elicit my confidences, to help the raincoats know my thoughts. I must ask nothing.

He thought of Joseph. As they walked, all three, into the glade where the picnic table stood, he stopped and turned to Prisbek. "You said that you have arranged that I may say mass here?"

"Yes, Your Eminence."

"Very well, then. I would like to say a mass this morning for the repose of my driver's soul. Can that be arranged?"

"Of course, Eminence."

"Then let us do it now."

5

The altar on which he had changed bread and wine into the body and blood of Christ was, in reality, the desk of some unknown pedagogue, facing a dusty green blackboard on which were scrawled remnants of chalk inscriptions. During the mass he had been, as always, oblivious to his surroundings, withdrawn

into the mystery and the miracle of the holy sacri-
fice. But now, as he genuflected before this makeshift altar and rose, saying the words that told his
meager audience that the mass was ended, he thought
of those masses said in prisons and concentration
camps by his fellow priests, so many of whom had
died in captivity during the long years of German
occupation. He had been a fifteen-year-old schoolboy when the first Soviet tanks arrived in the streets
of the capital, driving the Germans back, block by
razed block. While other boys of his generation re-
gretted that they had been too young to fight, he had
felt cheated of the honor of suffering imprisonment
and abuse in Christ's name. Now, remembering that
time, he turned to face his jailers, making the sign of
benediction, seeing among the scattered schoolroom
desks, Father Prisbek, who had served the mass,
and, kneeling midway down the room, the strange
nun. By the doorway, hunting rifles slung over their
shoulders, were the two men in loden coats and,
coming through the room, the Security Major. The
Security Major seemed distraught. He was looking
not at the altar, but at the blackboard behind it, and
now, seeing that he was watched, he forced a smile.
"A strange place for a religious service, Your Eminence."

"Not really. Masses are said in some of our
prisons, are they not?"

"I wouldn't know," the Security Major said,
moving past the makeshift altar to the blackboard.
He picked up a cloth duster. "This should have been
cleaned off for you," he said, with his false smile.
"We want to show you all respect."

What is on the blackboard that he wants to

hide? He watched the Major begin to rub the scrawls away. Only one was decipherable and he memorized it, seconds before the duster erased it.

27TH. 1200 HRS. RY. JASNA. SECTION 11

"If you are so anxious to show me respect," he said to the Security Major, "then you will find a way of putting me in touch with Minister Mazur."

The Major seemed pleased to hear this. "Indeed," he said. "I have just come to tell you that something has been arranged. If you will follow me, please."

"Father Prisbek?" The red-bearded priest came forward. He handed Prisbek his stole and untied the strings of the chasuble that Prisbek had provided. Then he followed the Major down through the scattered desks. This time, when they reached the hall, they did not go through the green baize door to Colonel Poulnikov's office, but upstairs, three flights to the top of the building.

There, in a large empty room like an attic, with sloping roofs and a dusty floor, the man called Colonel Poulnikov sat with another man on folding chairs, both of them hunched over a long table on which there were three field telephones, a shortwave radio transmitter and a metal box containing some unfamiliar electronic equipment. The Colonel stood up at once and made his old-fashioned formal bow. "Did you enjoy your walk, Your Eminence? Remember, if you have any complaints, I am here to help."

He ignored this. "What about the Minister?" he asked.

"Of course." The Colonel signaled to the other man behind the table. This man wore green rubber Wellington boots, muddied at the heels, brown corduroy leggings and a down-filled jacket, as though he had just come in from working in the fields. He cranked up the field telephone, then looked at a small monitor screen on the box of electronic equipment. "Just coming through," he said. He indicated a folding chair by the second field telephone. "Please, sit there."

There was a ringing sound. The man in Wellington boots picked up the first field telephone, listened, then pointed to the second phone. "Take that one, Your Eminence."

He did as he was told. Normally, when he telephoned from the Residence to the ministerial offices in Lubinova Street, his secretaries dealt with the ministerial secretaries and then, in a gesture of respect for the State, he allowed himself to be the one who waited, ready for that moment when the Minister picked up the phone. But now, as he lifted the receiver, someone was waiting for him. "Hello?" an unfamiliar voice said. "Hello?"

"Cardinal Bem speaking."

"Your Eminence, I am Starin, ministerial deputy. The Minister is in Gudno and may not be reached by telephone. A meeting of the Patriotic Clergy is in progress there. I have been empowered to act in his absence."

"Starin?" he said. "Have we met?"

"Yes, Your Eminence, but I doubt that you'd remember it."

All three men watched him—the Colonel, the Security Major, the man in Wellington boots—as he tried to put a face to the voice on the phone. "The April meeting, was it?"

"No, sir. As you'll recall that was a private meeting between yourself and the Minister."

"Yes, yes, so it was."

"We met before that, sir. But, as I said, it's not important. You wouldn't remember. Now sir, what is it that I can do for you?"

"I didn't ask to be brought here. I don't need 'protective custody.' My disappearance at this time will be a greater threat to stability than any so-called plot against my life."

"There is nothing 'so-called' about the plot against your life, sir. Someone has tried to kill you and we have reason to believe that they will try again."

"All right, then. Who's trying to kill me?"

"We don't know, sir. It's possible they may be Catholics who disagree with your policies."

"But that's ridiculous. Catholics trying to kill a Catholic priest? I'm afraid, Mr. Starin, that makes absolutely no sense."

As he spoke he saw the three men exchange glances. He did not understand the meaning of these glances. Then the voice on the telephone said, "Your Eminence, let me ask you a question. What would you do if you were told that in three days' time at the Jubilee celebrations at Rywald, the Church will announce that there is no longer a concordat between Church and State and that the time has come for the people of this country to openly defy the government in a demonstration of the national will?"

He stared at the watching faces. He realized they had turned up some dial on the electronic equipment that enabled them to hear Starin on the other end of the line. They too—the Colonel, the Major and the man in Wellingtons—waited his answer.

"If I were told such a thing," he said, "I would say this. I am the head of the Church in this country, and, as such, I am the only person empowered to present such a view. And I would reject any such statement publicly and at once."

He saw the watching faces again exchange covert glances. Then Starin said, "That is exactly our understanding, Your Eminence. And so, as you see, if there *is* such a plot, I mean a plot to use the Jubilee celebrations for counter-revolutionary ends, it would be necessary for them to remove you in advance."

"By killing me? The trouble with you people is you think that everyone would use the same means you do."

"Your Eminence, I have not finished. Supposing these people—fanatics—I don't say they represent the majority of the Catholics in this country— supposing these people—fanatics, as I said—killed you and then put out a false story about the killing."

"What false story?" This conversation was like a dream: in dreams the most improbable threats are heavy with fearful plausibility. And now the voice on the other end of the line spoke with dreamlike power.

"A false story that you have been killed by us— Internal Security—because we feared your sermon would be a call to open rebellion."

"But these people are *Catholics*."

"You said that before, Your Eminence. What about it?"

"Killing me would be a mortal sin."

"I'm not sure they would agree with you," said the voice on the phone. "Is the death of a traitor a mortal sin or an act of patriotism?"

The three men in the room watched him. The light blue eyes of Colonel Poulnikov fixed on him, unblinking, as though they were the eyes in a portrait. What shall I say? How can I convince them? "But I mustn't disappear," he said. "Especially if what you say is true. How can I help to prevent bloodshed if I am locked away here—on this farm or whatever you call it?"

As he said this the three men turned to each other and the Colonel nodded as though confirming something. At that moment there was a crackling sound on the telephone line. "Hello?" he said. "Hello, are you there?" But the line had gone dead. The man in Wellington boots picked up the other receiver, cranked the field telephone, then set the receiver back on its stand. "Call completed," he said to no one in particular.

"Call back," he told them. "I have not finished."

"I'm afraid they've terminated," the Colonel said. "There would be no point in ringing back."

"But it's important," he said. "Don't you realize that if there's going to be a rebellion, you will need my help?"

"I'm sorry," the Colonel said. "We'll just have to be content with that until further notice. Would you like to go back to your room?"

It was useless. He nodded his assent and the Security Major at once rose and came to him. The Major's face was inexplicably angry. "I'll see you back, then," the Major said, leading him to the door. As he went out, the Colonel rose and gave him a small farewell bow. The man in Wellington boots switched off the power on the electronics box.

As they started downstairs, the Major, walking ahead, turned and looked back up at him. "When I was a boy," the Major said, "I used to read about bad priests—you know, like those popes, the

Borgias, very corrupt people who were cruel and greedy. I asked my father about it and he said it was just Masonic propaganda—all lies. But I always wondered. I still do. What would make a man like you corrupt? Power?"

"Are you saying that I am corrupt?"

The Major paused on the staircase, then walked on down. "Yes," he said.

"And why do you think that?"

"I believe you will do anything to keep your power. To remain as head of the Church here."

They had reached the first landing and now went down a second flight. He looked at the top of the Major's brilliantined head, one step below him. "No wonder you Communists cannot understand our people," he said. "You see everything through your own distorting mirror."

"Do we?" the Major asked. "What does Your Eminence mean by that?"

"I mean that power is your preoccupation, not mine."

They reached the bottom of the second flight of stairs and the Major preceded him along the corridor that led to his room. The Major opened the door, which was not locked, then stood in the doorway, waiting for him to go in.

"So you're not interested in power," the Major said. "I can't believe that. What would you like me to think? That you want to be a saint and a martyr, is that it?"

"I am here on earth to serve God. That and only that."

"Rubbish," the Major said. "Your religion isn't even skin-deep. You're a careerist, that's what you are."

"I hope you are mistaken."

The Major smiled, an angry smile. "No, I don't think so." He turned away, leaving the door open. "Lunch will be at two o'clock," he said. "We'll come for you."

6

Somewhere in the unseen kitchens a radio played dance music, a prewar tune that he remembered from his school days. Back there, the clatter of plates indicated that at least two people were at work. At a long trestle table in the school dining room he and Father Prisbek sat alone while, at the other end, the guards, their rifles propped beside their benches, spooned out portions of red cabbage. At a facing trestle table the Colonel, the Security Major and the man in Wellingtons served themselves from a tureen of boiled potatoes that they then passed over to Prisbek. The nun came from the kitchens carrying a platter of little sausages. As she passed him by she said, "If you will wait a moment, Your Eminence, we have some boiled eggs for you. I know you don't eat spicy things. These are spicy."

"I know they are spicy," he said. "Karamalinker sausages. My favorites. I'll have some."

"Are you sure?"

"Of course. I told you, I'm no longer on a diet."

The Colonel said, "Karamalinker sausages. First-class. My favorite, also."

"I like the Dalancas," said the man in Wellingtons. "You know, with thin skins. They talk about that Polish sausage—what's its name?—Debreciners—but it's not a patch on our Dalancas."

"Like Polish ham," the Colonel said. "It can't compare with our ham, especially the sweet ham from Gallina. Gallina ham is known to connoisseurs."

"The best ham in the world," the Security Major said. "Am I right, Eminence?"

He nodded, watching the man in Wellingtons greedily slather mustard on his sausages. Why do small nations like ours boast of trivial achievements: our world-famous ham, our ice hockey team? "And what about our music, our literature?" he said, looking directly at the Colonel. "We were known for that, once."

"We still are," the Colonel said. "Stanislaus Lork won the Vienna International Prize for Literature—when was it?—last year?—the year before last?"

There was a sudden silence at the table. He saw the Security Major bow his head as though someone had mentioned a death.

"Of course," the Colonel said, recovering, "he's not the best example. His work's been judged decadent."

"Decadent? I don't know about that," the man in Wellingtons said, reaching for the pickle jar. "I mean, I don't read fiction and poetry and that stuff. But I do know I don't like people who run away to the West when the going gets rough."

"Lork didn't run away," Father Prisbek said heatedly. "He was *driven* out."

"Well, whatever," said the man in Wellingtons.

"What is he now but one of those lapdogs of the West? I mean those exile artists sitting around in Paris or New York, talking about their sufferings while the rest of us—" He stopped in midsentence. "How did we get onto this subject?" he said, angrily.

The Security Major, who had been silent, said in low tones, "The Cardinal brought it up. You went to Jesuit school, didn't you, Your Eminence?"

"Yes," he said. "And so did your prime minister."

"Did he?" The Colonel looked surprised. At that point the nun came again from the unseen kitchens. "Who wants some boiled eggs?" she asked. "I made them for His Eminence, but if any of you gentlemen . . . ?"

The Colonel shook his head and wiped his mouth with a paper napkin. "It's fourteen-fifty," he said to the man in Wellingtons. Both rose at once.

"You may take him for another walk if he wants to go," the Colonel said to Prisbek. Then he, the Major and the man in Wellingtons went out.

"Well, do any of the rest of you want these eggs?" the nun asked.

One of the armed guards put up his hand.

7

At four o'clock, as he finished vespers in the room that he now thought of as his cell, he heard a car engine outside. He went to the window and saw, below in the yard, the Colonel and the man in Wellingtons climbing into a muddy farm truck in the back of which were several long planks of the sort used by builders. The Colonel shouted something that he did not hear and one of the men in loden coats opened the farmyard gate. The truck drove out.

It had been raining. The cobblestones in the yard were wet. Above him, roaring loud over the building, a large plane came down through clouds, moving lower as on a landing approach. He saw that it was a Russian Aeroflot airliner. As the plane noise diminished, someone knocked on his door.

"Yes?"

The door opened. Father Prisbek. He wore a yellow slicker of the type used on sailing boats and carried a similar slicker, which he offered, saying, "They gave me these. Would you like to go for your walk now?"

"Outside the walls?"

"Yes," Prisbek said. "They have no objection."

"Very well, then." He took the slicker and followed Prisbek downstairs. There was no one in sight in the hall or in the adjoining rooms. Prisbek opened the front door and they crossed the yard, where the men in loden coats opened the gate for them as they had done, moments before, for the Colonel's truck.

"Do you think it's going to rain again?" Prisbek asked one of the men as they passed through the gate.

The man replied, "Don't worry. Won't be more than a shower."

They walked down the track that led to the woods. No one seemed to follow them. He looked covertly at Prisbek, noticing that Prisbek's skin was mottled with eczema under the sparse red beard. He remembered the heated way Prisbek had spoken up, defending Lork, the writer who had chosen exile. Can I trust him?

"Tell me," he asked Prisbek. "Are you, by chance, one of the Patriotic Clergy?"

Prisbek stopped walking and turned to stare. "You're joking, surely, Eminence?"

"Well, the thought crossed my mind. As you know, the Patriotic Clergy work closely with the government."

"They are traitors," Prisbek said. "I'm surprised that you'd think for a moment that I was one of those scum."

"Then why are you here?"

"I was brought here. I was asked to act as your chaplain and I agreed. I thought it would help you."

"But you must know that *I* appoint my chaplains."

Prisbek hesitated. "Yes, of course," he said. "But you can't expect *them* to know that, can you?"

He looked again at Prisbek as they continued on toward the wood. "There is something about this that puzzles me," he said. "Why are we allowed to walk alone, outside the walls? There are guards but they are not guarding us. Why is that, do you think?"

Prisbek hunched his shoulders in an odd, defensive movement. "They told me it would be useless to try to run away. We are in the middle of nowhere. That's what the Colonel said."

"Are we? A few minutes ago a Russian airliner came in on a landing pattern. We can't be far from the city."

"Do you think so?" Prisbek said.

"Yes. And if that is the case, there must be a main road near here."

"I don't know. Look, Your Eminence. I don't want to be negative, but I don't see how we could get away. For one thing, we have no transport."

They had now entered the wood and were walking along the path that led to the abandoned picnic table. "Nevertheless," he said, "I intend to try."

He quickened his pace. As he did he put on the yellow slicker, thinking: This will make me look less like a priest. With Prisbek behind him he went past the picnic table and, leaving the path, struggled through thick underbrush. Two crows, cawing in alarm, rose up from the trees at his approach. He could hear Prisbek panting behind him. Incongruously, he remembered a lecture he had given last winter, urging the clergy to take more exercise and keep their bodies fit. This man was half his age. He went on. Ahead, he saw the edge of the wood and, beyond it, a plowed field. They emerged into this field and looked around. Some blackbirds rose from the furrows and flew away. He looked across the field, then turned to Prisbek, who stood, panting, his head swinging wildly this way and that as though searching for an enemy.

"Well, Prisbek. What do you think? Will we make a run for it?"

"Where?" Prisbek said, showing his palms in a gesture of hopelessness. "Where are we?"

"Look," he said, pointing. At the far end of the field was a small secondary road, not a farm track, but a paved surface. He began to walk, half running across the plowed field, his shoes sinking into the soft earth. He heard Prisbek coming up behind him. He went on, out in the open now, half expecting a rifle shot.

"Eminence, I really think we should go back."

"Why? What are you? Are you a priest or a policeman?"

"We should go back!" Prisbek said. He seemed hysterical. "My God, do you want to be shot?"

"If it's God's will, I will be shot," he said. "In the meantime, let's decide. Which direction will we take?"

They had reached the secondary road. He stopped and looked at the wood, trying to determine in which direction the plane had come down on its approach.

"Please," Prisbek said. "Your Eminence, listen to me. They're going to find us. And when they bring us back they'll lock us up and keep us locked up. It would be easier if we go back now."

"Do what you want," he told Prisbek. "I'm going this way." He pointed down the road, then started walking. After a minute he heard footsteps behind him. Is he following as my jailer or my ally? Why are we free? Or, are we free?

He went on. Ahead, high on the slope of a hill, was a small farm building with smoke coming from its chimney and, in the rough yard in front, a horse, grazing. It was the only sign of human habitation on either side of the road. He looked back, seeing Prisbek hurrying along several paces in the rear. All was quiet, rural, drowsy—a warm summer's afternoon. Suddenly, there was a flurry ahead of him as two black-faced sheep ran off the road, scrambling through a gap in a hedge to retreat into a cornfield. So there is little traffic on this road. He thought of the muddy farm truck in which the Colonel and the man in Wellingtons had driven off, a truck loaded with builders' wooden planks. Why would the Security forces travel in such a vehicle if it were not to deceive the people of this region? They do not want anyone to know about my being here. Then, why are we allowed to walk along this road?

"Eminence! Eminence!"

Prisbek, fifty yards back down the road, was now sitting on the edge of the ditch, holding his thigh as though he were in pain.

"What's wrong?"

"My knee. I twisted something."

Is it a trick? But if Prisbek is really in pain it's shameful to abandon him. Reluctantly he went back to the red-bearded priest. "Can you walk? Come, I'll help you."

Awkwardly, Prisbek tried to rise and stand, but, wincing, sat down again. "No, you go on," he said. "I'll stay here."

"I don't like to leave you."

Prisbek looked up and said in a surprisingly bitter tone, "Leave me, leave me. It doesn't matter to you. You got me into this."

"Yes," he said. "Yes, I suppose I did." He stood for a moment, considering. "If you can't walk," he said, "I'll go on and see if I can get some help."

"Help?" Prisbek said. "What help? Go on, go on. Leave me. Good-bye, Your Eminence."

"I'll do my best," he said and turned away. The road stretched ahead empty and silent. Why do I feel like Judas leaving this man who may himself be

———

a Judas-goat brought here to trap me? Simple charity should demand that I do not condemn Prisbek when I do not know his motive. Help me, O Lord.

As always, in prayer, in the act of prayer, he sought to open that inner door to the silence of God, God who waited, watched and judged. He thought ahead to the Jubilee celebrations next Tuesday, to the thousands and thousands of pilgrims who would come to Rywald and climb the Jasna mountain to the church, built two hundred years ago to honor the September Martyrs. There in that place dedicated to God, a concatenation of events could be set in motion destroying all his gains: the right to have church schools, the right to publish religious literature, the right to worship freely, the right to build churches in the new territories. All of that would disappear. Instead, there would be tanks in the streets, torture in secret rooms, prisons overflowing, riots, beatings, deaths. Help me, O Lord. Let me be in Rywald on that day. I must be seen. I must be heard.

8

In the quiet of this place the only sound had been the cawing of the crows and his footsteps on the road. But a noise, becoming louder, made him look up. Ahead, around a bend in the road, came a small car, traveling slowly. He stopped. The car came on.

On the roof he saw a round object. A searchlight. Police, not the Security Police, who traveled in unmarked blue Ladas, but the ordinary police, their vehicle marked plainly with the red, blue and yellow insignia of the State, the sort of police car one might meet on any highway. He began to walk again, pulling his yellow slicker tight about his neck to hide his priestly collar. There were two uniformed police in the car. He quickened his pace. Should he nod to them as they passed by?

Twenty yards away, the car's searchlight went on, flashing red in the late afternoon sun. The car stopped. One of the policemen got out, pointing to him, signaling him to stay where he was. The policeman then approached, casually, holding out his hand with the air of a man in command. "Papers?"

In his jacket pocket he kept, always, a small worn wallet containing a photograph of his dead mother, a doctor's certificate listing his blood type and medical history and the plastic-covered identity card issued to all citizens. If they are already searching for me it is useless to resist. But if this is a normal police check, my card tells nothing but my Christian name and surname, birthplace and age. He took the card from his wallet but as he did he was forced to open his yellow slicker, revealing his collar to the policeman's gaze. The policeman looked at the card and returned it, saying, "What are you doing here?"

"My car broke down." He was surprised to hear himself lie so easily.

"Where?"

"A couple of miles back."

"Where were you going?"

"I don't know. We were lost."

"We? Who's we?"

It was too late to cover up the slip. Besides, Prisbek was injured and needed help. "Myself and another priest."

"Where's the other one?"

"Down the road a bit. He hurt his knee and can't walk."

"Get in the car," the policeman said. "There— in the back."

He did as he was told. The policeman sat in the front seat beside the driver. "There's a second one down the road," the policeman said to the driver. The car started off slowly. He stared ahead. Was Prisbek hiding in the ditch? The car, moving on, passed the place where Prisbek had been. A hundred yards further on he told them to stop. "Here," he said. "I left him here."

The car pulled in to the side of the road and the first policeman got out, climbed to the top of the ditch and looked over the hedge at the fields beyond. He then jumped down and walked back to the car. "Where is he?"

"I don't know."

"Sure this is where you left him?"

"May I look?"

The policeman nodded.

He got out of the car and climbed the ditch. Across the expanse of plowed field was the edge of the wood that bordered on the false agricultural school. There was no sign of Prisbek. He had lied about his knee so that he could go back and tell them. He could reach the cover of those woods in a few minutes.

"Well?" the policeman called out.

"I don't know," he said, climbing down onto the road again. "Maybe he went back to our car. I don't know."

"Get in," the policeman said. As he climbed back into the rear seat, he heard the driver say, "It's four-fifty. If we look for the other one we'll miss roll call."

"You're right," the first policeman said. "All right, let's go back. I'll put it on the radio."

"No, wait awhile." The driver reversed the car, then, speeding up, drove off, going away from the direction of the wood. "If you put it on the radio now," he said to the other policeman, "they could tell us to go find him. Let's wait and radio closer to town."

"Hey, that's right," the policeman said. He then slued around and looked back, grinning. "Your name is Stephen. That's my name, too."

"Then we have the same saint's day," he said.

"That's right," the policeman said. "My ma used to have a picnic for us kids on that day. What's your other name?"

"Peter."

"No. I mean your surname. It was on the card. I forgot."

He felt his throat constrict. "Bem," he said.

The driver said, "Bem? Hey, that's the name of the Cardinal. You know. Your boss."

"That's right," he said. "It's a common enough name."

"Bem's from the Biala district, isn't he?" the driver said. "Yes, I think he's from Biala."

It could have been a trap but he did not think

so. They were ordinary policemen patrolling on an ordinary road. Or perhaps they were patrolling to keep people away from that false agricultural school? "No, he's not from Biala," he said. "He's from the city, same as me."

They drove on in silence for a while. Then the driver said, "You're in deep shit, Father."

"Why is that?"

"This is a restricted area." The driver turned to the other policeman. "Didn't you tell him?"

"Not yet."

"Why did the other one run away, Father?" the driver asked him.

"He didn't run away."

"Try telling that to Commandant Majewska."

"I told you," he said. "Our car broke down and his knee was hurting. He probably went back to sit in the car."

But the policemen seemed to have lost interest. They had begun to fiddle with the radio and now a voice announced, "One–nothing at the half. And they're coming out again. Yes, Danielski's back! He's all right. Yes!"

"Danielski! Hey!" the first policeman said. "Watch out, Belgium."

Football. He remembered that the World Cup was on this week. The policemen listened as play began and he thought again of Prisbek. So he *is* on their side. When he tells them I've gone, will they notify the local police to be on the lookout for me? If so, when these men radio in, that will be the end of it.

But almost at the moment he thought this, the driver switched the radio off. The commentator's voice died to silence. The policemen stared ahead, suddenly watchful. A vehicle was approaching, a mud-spattered truck. At first he was not sure, but then saw the builders' planks sticking out.

"Who are they?" one of the policemen asked.

"It's the Ostrof Farm School people," the other said. "They're all right."

The truck came closer. In the front were the Colonel and the man in Wellingtons. Instinctively, he lowered his head, concealing his face by putting his hand over his forehead. They are coming back from wherever they went earlier. They do not know about me. *They do not know.*

As the truck drew level, the policemen, losing interest in it, switched the radio on again. The football commentator cried, "Kroch has the ball and passes to Damon. Damon coming down left center."

The truck passed by, close on the narrow road. He did not see it pass, as he had turned his head away from that side of the road. His body felt as though he were trembling, but he was not.

"Now it's Danielski moving up on Damon, he's got the ball—brilliant!—yes, he has it now, oh, that footwork, he's through the Belgian defense, it's wide open. He—yes! He scores!"

"Hey, he did it!" the policemen yelled in unison. Slowly, cringing as though he would be attacked, he risked a look back through the rear window of the police car. The truck was two hundred yards away, going toward a turn in the road. "What a scene!" the commentator said. "The teammates crowding around, the fans in the stands going wild. It's a great moment here in Cherny Stadium!"

Abruptly, one of the policemen lowered the

---

sound. "Shit," he said, in a worried voice. "I just thought. If we call in that we picked up one priest and there's another still loose in the restricted area, Majewska's going to have our balls. We're supposed to radio in as soon as we contact a suspect and wait for further instructions."

"Right," the other policeman said. "And once he has us in violation, then it's a written report."

"Shit."

They switched the radio volume up and again he heard the roar of the football crowd, the excited tones of the commentator. But he saw that the policemen were using the noise as a cover for their whispering together in the front seat. At last, decided, they leaned back listening to the game.

The landscape, hilly, empty, with no other roads, gradually began to change. Ahead, the road dipped in a series of winding curves and below, in a valley, he saw a small town, little more than a village, a few streets, a square, a church spire, a main street trailing off to nothingness. The church spire was typical of the smaller churches in his diocese and the roofs of the houses were in the German style common to his part of the country. They reached the first intersecting road and slowed down as a group of men rode by on bicycles, carrying steel lunch pails and wearing helmets with flashlamps attached. He recognized them as miners. Then, as they came to the first streets, the police car slowed down, the policemen shutting off the car radio, driving as though searching for something. Slowing almost to a stop, the car turned up a narrow hilly lane, going toward a place that looked like a refuse dump. The driver pulled in and parked on the rim of a steep quarry. At the foot of the quarry great piles of garbage sat like ruined buildings. Gulls, wheeling and searching, moved in a restless flock over this miasma of trash. The policeman who was not driving leaned back and opened the rear door of the car.

"All right, Father. Get out."

Were they going to shoot him? Why should they shoot him? They were ordinary policemen on ordinary patrol. They didn't know anything about him.

But he hesitated. Suddenly he felt afraid. "Why?" he asked.

The driver said, "Because I was an altar boy, that's why!" The other policeman laughed.

"No, I'm joking," the driver said. "We're giving you a chance. Don't ask why. We do something for you, you do something for us. We never picked you up. You never saw us. You walked all the way here to report that your car broke down. You didn't know you were driving in a restricted area. I'm not saying we believe you. But it doesn't matter now."

"Wait," the other policeman said. "If I was you, Father, I wouldn't report that you left your car back there. I'd say nothing. I'd just try to get home. All right? Now, get out."

He eased himself out of the backseat and stood. The car door slammed. The little car swerved in a U-turn and drove off down the lane. He was alone with the circling gulls, looking down into the wasteland quarry with its ghost streets of ill-smelling detritus. It was as though he had been cast down here, abandoned, stripped of the rank and privileges he had known these many years. He was now a hunted man, sought by forces of the State who had tried to imprison him. He stared down into the bleak gull-haunted canyon. Into his mind like a half-forgotten incantation came the words: *Pro nomine Jesu contumelias pati*. To suffer in Jesus' name. That is now my fate and I must give thanks for it. My task is to serve You. For that task I must be free.

9

His hand went to his collar and unhooked it, pulling it off. He also removed the purple shirtfront that proclaimed his episcopal rank. Wrapping the white Roman collar in the purple linen, he threw them both down into the canyon of trash, watching them separate and fall among the wheeling, eddying gulls. He buttoned the yellow slicker around his throat and, remembering, slipped his episcopal ring from his finger and put it in his trouser pocket. He turned and walked down the narrow lane that led to the highway.

I must find a telephone. But the secretariat telephones will be tapped. If I call I will simply be telling the SP where to find me. And if, as the Security Colonel said, I have enemies within the Church itself, I could, by revealing my whereabouts, offer them another chance to assassinate me.

At once, he thought of Jan Ley. With Jan I will have no need to identify myself. He knows my voice, knows my thoughts, my fears, my doubts. Perhaps I can telephone him from this town.

Several minutes later he reached the highway and saw ahead a garage and a yard filled with butane gas cylinders. The garage was closed, the gasoline pumps seemed disused, but in a nearby yard, a young man was loading a butane cylinder onto the back of a rusty iron dolly. He went up to him. "Excuse me," he said. "My car broke down a few miles away. I'm afraid I'm lost. Where is this place?"

"This place? Ricany," the young man said.

"Thank you. Do you have a telephone?"

"No. No telephone."

"Thank you," he said again. He went on. He had been right about the miners. Ricany was a coal-mining village about two hundred kilometers from the capital. He tried to remember if he knew any names of local clergy, but, of course, he did not. He had always been bad at remembering names and Ricany was not the sort of place much mentioned in diocesan affairs.

As he walked down the main street he saw one of the new free markets that the State had agreed to permit, a hodgepodge of outdoor stalls selling everything from used clothing to rock cassettes. Further on was the village square and the town hall, a Renaissance building with an ornate clock tower that announced the time as five-twenty. On the side wall of the town hall was a gaudy red banner, proclaiming Soviet Friendship Week and advertising a Russian circus, free to all. He noticed that the date coincided with Tuesday's celebrations at Rywald. He was not surprised. It had been planned that way. It was a measure of the government's unease. In his ten years as bishop and seven as cardinal he had seen the power of the State erode while the Church, despite its mistakes, had assumed greater and greater power over people's minds. The Party had unwittingly strengthened that power by stripping the Church of its prewar estates and leaving it as poor as the people themselves. And yet, as he knew, this churchly power was not real. It was the sort of power that he, as cardinal, would have held in the sixteenth century. In those days the Cardinal became the head of State in the interregnum between the death of one king and the coronation of his successor.

Today I rule in a similar vacuum. Not because the people love God, but because they fear their leaders. God's kingdom cannot be of this world. That is why I walk these streets as a fugitive.

At that moment he saw, rising from the squat red German roofs of this place, a narrow spire surmounted by a cross. It seemed a sign. He hurried through the crowded stalls of the outdoor market, instinctively lowering his head so as not to be recognized. But as he passed the shouting hucksters, the drably dressed men and women picking among sparse displays of American-style jeans, used winter coats, Bulgarian shoes, photographs and posters of foreign film stars, toy pistols and miscellaneous automobile parts, no one looked at him, no older woman gave him the respectful nod with which that generation saluted the presence of a priest. He, who as cardinal had rarely walked unaccompanied, who was accustomed to the help of assistants in finding a shortcut to a platform, a car waiting at the exit, who had long grown used to the fact that his crimson sash attracted stares, now looked into blank faces as though he had become invisible.

He went on, watching the spire ahead. He turned into a narrow lane where faded graffiti urged solidarity for the miners' strike of two years ago. And now he saw two policemen approaching. He stopped, confused. But the policemen passed him by. He crossed a roundabout and saw the church directly ahead, a smallish building at the end of the lane. At the entrance was a notice board giving the hours of services and some diocesan notices. He stopped to study them. Sometimes such notices would indicate if the pastor was a member of the Organization of Patriotic Clergy, by advertising special government rallies and meetings organized by the Ministry for Religious Affairs. There were none on this board and yet, as he entered the church, he felt a certain unease. He dipped his fingers in the worn marble font and pushed open the heavy old leather-bound door leading into the nave.

Candles were lit at a side altar. He genuflected. Some sort of novena was in progress and there was exposition of the Blessed Sacrament on the main altar. Women were arranging flowers in vases and carrying them to the altar. About twenty people, including youths and some workmen, knelt in prayer before the bright candles, the flowers, the Host in its ornate gold-and-silver monstrance. It was a scene that might have been staged to comfort and reassure him. And yet as he knelt at the rear of the church he was filled with a feeling he had never known before under God's roof. It was as though he were watched and at any moment a hand would be placed on his shoulder and he would be led outside. Yet there was nothing in this scene to prompt such alarm.

Suddenly, he heard loud footsteps coming up the aisle on his left. He looked over. The man in the side aisle was heavily built, wearing a bulky red cardigan darned at the elbows. His hair was silvery, his face seamed with years. He watched as this man went through the gate at the altar rail and entered the sacristy through a door at the side of the main altar. So he is the sexton. Or the priest. If he is the priest it's unlikely that he will be Patriotic Clergy. Men of his age in a place like this have found their niche. They are not greedy for further powers.

Will I risk it? Will I follow him into the sacristy and speak to him, tell him who I am and ask his help in reaching Father Ley?

He rose, genuflected, then walked up the side aisle going to the altar rail. The ladies who were arranging the altar flowers at a side table within the altar area were now quite close to him. One of them walked across the altar steps, genuflected to the Host and placed a vase of gladioli at the left-hand side of the altar. He waited, not wishing to disturb her by entering the altar area before she had finished her task. As he did, he noticed that she walked with a limp. Then as she passed him, coming down the altar steps, he saw her face, marked by tiny cuts. He caught his breath. But she did not look at him. She went to the side table and, picking up the wrapping paper and the discarded leaves of the gladioli, turned and went in through the sacristy door at the side of the altar.

Quickly he genuflected and went back down the aisle to the rear of the church, pushing the leather-bound door open, forgetting to dip his hand in holy water and make the sign of the cross as he left the church. He felt sweat on his brow and, suddenly, there were damp patches under his armpits. He began to walk quickly, not aware of his direction. She is in there, decorating the altar, a sodality lady, pious, lonely, her life centered around devotions and good works. The Security Colonel was right. They are Catholics. Catholics who want to kill me.

10

The rich aroma of espresso coffee brought back a memory of those coffee shops that rose like small miracles of luxury in the ruined streets of the capital in the first postwar years. A penniless seminarian then, he would inhale its odor and look in wonderingly at the refrigerated trays of meringues and napoleons, sacher torte and macaroons, at the tables crowded with stylish young matrons in felt boots and mannish hats, at Russian officers and foreigners from the Western embassies. Now, in the warm late afternoon sun as he walked down the main street of this little town, he inhaled that half-forgotten aroma and paused by an open door, remembering that former time.

But, on inspection, this coffee shop revealed itself as very different from his memories. A few scattered biscuits and an insipid cream cake sat solitary on a counter while behind the empty trays a woman in a white coat arranged ordinary loaves of bread on a shelf. The place was almost empty. A waitress placed a glass of water and a minuscule cup of coffee before the sole customer, a bald man who wore a blue, short-sleeved shirt and smoked a cigar. Somewhere in the background a turntable played a Strauss waltz.

"Is there a telephone?" he asked the woman behind the counter.

She pointed. "In the back."

As he walked past the empty tables, going toward the kitchen and toilets, the man with the cigar turned and stared at him. But the man was alone and probably bored. Still, when he picked up the receiver in the small back hallway beside the kitchen, he decided to speak in a whisper. He began to dial; then, looking at the machine, realized how out of touch he was with the details of ordinary life. For, of course, it was a pay telephone. He replaced the receiver and went back to the bakery counter. As he proffered his hundred-droschen note and asked the woman behind the counter if she would make change, two young men came into the shop. Both were in their early twenties and wore jeans and cotton T-shirts. This did not reassure him. Kris Malik had told him that young men and girls, informally dressed, were employed by the SP to loiter in public places and listen to what was said. The young men glanced at him as they sat down at a table near the door. He took his change and went back to the pay telephone. He dialed the familiar number and an operator told him how much he should put in the machine. After a moment he heard the phone ring in that gray Jesuit house that sat on a hillside overlooking the Volya River. "Is Father Ley there?"

"Who shall I say is calling?"

His own name came half out of his mouth before he remembered. "Tell him," he said, "tell him, it's Tonio."

"Tonio?"

"Yes."

Tonio had been his nickname in the days when he and Jan Ley studied theology at "the Greg"— Gregorian University in Rome. Jan was the only person in this country who knew him by that name. He waited. Jan was lame and his room was far from the phone. As he waited he wondered about that other person who listened in the dead telephonic lull. Then he heard a jarring sound in his ear as someone, fumbling, picked up the telephone receiver from the shelf where it had been laid.

"Tonio, come stai? E dove stai?"

"I'm well, Father," he said. He did not think it wise that they speak Italian. To the listener it would seem suspicious and, of course, the tape could be quickly translated. "Tell me," he said. "Have you had any word from Cardinal Bem?"

"Word about what?" Jan asked.

"Our petition, Father. Do you know, by any chance, if he's still in the city? Maybe he's away. Maybe that's why we haven't heard from him."

"It's funny you should say that, Tonio. Would you believe it, the gentlemen in raincoats rang up not an hour ago wanting to know when was the last time I spoke to the Cardinal. When I asked them why, they said: 'Well, he seems to have disappeared.' "

"Disappeared?"

"Yes, the whole thing's very strange. I've just spoken to Father Finder, one of his secretaries. He says the raincoats themselves came to the Cardinal's

Residence last night and took him into what they call 'protective custody.' They claimed someone was trying to kill him. What do you make of that, Tonio?"

"Me?" he said. "What would I know about such things? All I know is, if the Cardinal's been arrested, we're not going to get an answer to our petition."

"True enough," Jan said. "Well, is there anything else I can do for you, Tonio?"

"Well, yes," he said. "I wonder if I could have a small loan. Maybe a thousand droschen, if you could spare it."

"Of course. Where shall I send it?"

"I'm hoping to come into the city. Are you still hearing confessions at Santa Maria?"

"Every morning, from seven o'clock till nine."

"Good. Well, perhaps I can come tomorrow. And Father? I need your advice on a spiritual matter."

"I'll be there. With your money."

"Thank you, Father."

"*Ciao, Tonio. A domani.*"

"*Ciao, Giannino,*" he said.

As he put the receiver back on its cradle the kitchen door banged open and the young waitress he had seen earlier came out, carrying several glasses of ice water on a tray. "Sorry, sir. Were you wanting to order something?"

"No, thank you."

He followed her undulating hips as she went into the café, deciding as he threaded his way past the empty tables that it would be better to ask directions from someone else. The young men in jeans were playing dominoes. The man in the blue shirt eyed the waitress as she passed.

When he reached the street outside, he looked up and down, searching for a sign that might indicate that an interurban bus stopped here. There was no sign. He stood there, indecisive; an old woman came toward him carrying a dingy cloth carrier bag. As she drew level with him she opened it, revealing a mound of cherries inside. "Yes, sir," she said, giving him a complicit smile. "These are from my allotment. Just picked."

He shook his head, declining the transaction. "Tell me," he asked. "Is there a bus or train station in this town?"

"The train station is on Kocharna, sir. Next street over." She pointed to the cross street. "These cherries," she said, "I want to get rid of them tonight. I'll sell them cheap."

"Another time," he told her. "And thank you, madam."

Suddenly her mouth split in a lizardlike grin, showing that most of her teeth were gone. "You look like somebody—some gentleman, sir. Who is it they tell you you look like?"

"Oh, no one," he said. He waved a farewell to her in what, belatedly, he realized was his gesture of blessing. He had better get off the streets as quickly as possible. There was every chance that the alarm was out by now. Certainly the Colonel and his people would be on the roads, searching. He walked down to the cross street she had indicated and saw ahead what was surely the rail station, a turn-of-the-century Germanic brick building, its once ornate cornices and columns partially concealed by a "modernized" security entrance of wood-and-glass panels, built so that searches could be conducted before travelers were allowed to enter the station proper. He went toward it cautiously, but saw that there was no one on duty in the security hut. As he passed through into the station he saw, coming toward him, two soldiers carrying Kalashnikov automatic rifles. He stopped, feeling himself start to tremble. Then, into his mind, stilling the trembling, came words. *I am not alone. He is with me.* He walked on. The soldiers glanced at him but did not stop him.

11

The station seemed deserted. The arrivals board was blank, the newspaper kiosk shut. The only people on the platform were a mountain family dressed in traditional garb, as though they had been brought there for some folk festival of dance and singing. The men wore wide-brimmed shepherd's hats with trailing colored ribbons and smoked long clay pipes, from time to time spitting jets of tobacco juice on the tracks below. The women, bulky in traditional waistcoats and embroidered skirts, cast their eyes down modestly as he went past them. Only one ticket booth was open. He went up to it. The girl behind the wicket sat flipping the pages of an illustrated color magazine that contained pictures of film stars. The text was in a language that she obviously did not understand. The language was German. He had time to notice this because she turned several pages before acknowledging his presence. At last, she looked up.

"Yes?"

"When is the next train for the city, please?"

"Ten o'clock."

"Nothing before? Is there, perhaps, a bus, please, miss?"

"This is a train station," she said. "I don't sell bus tickets. Do you want a train ticket?"

"Well, it's a long wait till ten o'clock. If you could tell me where I might find out if there's a bus, I would be grateful."

"Ask opposite the town hall." She turned a page in the illustrated magazine, then looked up again. "Next, please."

"I'm sorry." He turned, realizing that someone was waiting behind him, but as he did the person behind him said, quickly, "Yes, there is a bus," and touched him on the shoulder. "Come. I'll show you."

He turned around. The person was Prisbek. He was no longer dressed in his cassock but wore a cream cotton jacket, a plaid sports shirt and black clerical trousers. "This way," Prisbek said, leading him away from the ticket window.

He looked down the station. The mountain family still sat on their bundles, the soldiers still marched up and down near the entrance. And then, coming from behind the boarded-up newspaper kiosk, a new figure entered the scene, wearing a cocoa-colored straw hat of the sort used by American tourists. "Ah, there you are," the Security Major said. "Good evening, Eminence."

He tried to disengage himself from Prisbek's grip but did not succeed. "So you are working for the Security Police?" he said to Prisbek. "You're one of Father Bialy's men, aren't you?"

"Bialy?" Prisbek said. "I told you before. I've nothing to do with the Patriotic Clergy. You're probably a closer friend to Bialy than ever I was."

The Security Major now took hold of his other arm. "Never mind all that," the Major said. "Just come this way."

It seemed foolish to try to make a fight of it. They were younger and stronger than he. They led him through the security hut and out into the street. When they reached the street a red Volvo pulled out a block away and drove up to meet them. The driver, who wore a loden coat, was one of the guards from the Ostrof farm.

The Major opened the rear door of the Volvo. "Get in, please."

He hesitated. "Please?" the Major said. "There's no point in making a fuss."

He got in. Prisbek sat in front with the driver. "Take a left," the Major told the driver. "And then a left again."

"We're not going back, then?" the driver asked.

"No, I think not. I've sent for Section Two. Left, that's it. Now left again and straight on."

The Volvo was now proceeding slowly down an alleyway past the back doors of small dwellings. "Here we are," the Major said, pointing to a doorway. "Pull in there."

The Volvo stopped. Looking through the rear window, he saw that they were not far from the town hall and about a block from the steeple of the church. The Major leaned over and took a radio transmitter from the glove compartment of the car.

"Section Two," he said into the transmitter. "We are at five point with livestock. Repeat five point. Over."

He replaced the transmitter. "Tell me," he said. "How did you get into town so quickly?"

He looked at the Major. So the policemen had not reported picking him up. "I walked," he said.

"No, no, Eminence," the Major said. "*Somebody* picked you up. I wonder who. I wonder what you told them. I wonder. But you're not going to tell *me*, of course. Father Prisbek says that when he was going back through the wood he saw a police car on the road."

"Did he?" He turned to Prisbek, who sat silent in the front seat. "How is your knee, Father?" he said. "Better, I notice."

"You shouldn't have tried to run away," Prisbek said. "If I'd followed you, it wouldn't have made any difference. I told you. You can't get away."

The muddy farm truck had just pulled in behind them. It was driven by the man in Wellington boots. Colonel Poulnikov got out and came over. "Thank God," he said. "Where did you find him?"

"In the train station," the Major said. "Trying to buy a ticket to the city."

"Who gave him the lift?" the Colonel asked.

"He hasn't told us that yet. Have you, Eminence?"

"Nor will I," he said.

"He probably telephoned someone when he arrived in Ricany," the Colonel said. "His people, or whoever. Which rules out going back to the farm. A pity."

"There's Moldova," the Major said.

"It will have to be that, then."

"What about Sister Martha?" Prisbek asked.

The Colonel nodded. "I've been in touch. They're on their way."

The Colonel then went back and sat in his truck. But the truck did not move out. Both vehicles sat for several minutes and, at last, a station wagon entered the alley. He recognized it as the same one they had used when they took him from Lazienca Street. The driver he did not know: a gray-haired man wearing a Security Policeman's shiny raincoat. Beside him sat a man in a loden jacket: the other guard from the farm. The middle-aged nun was in the backseat. As soon as the station wagon entered the alley, the Colonel's truck started up its engine. A small procession then drove out of the alley, the Colonel's truck in front, the Volvo next and the station wagon bringing up the rear. They went up the main street and at a crossroads they left the town of Ricany.

They were now on a main highway but he did not know in which direction they were traveling. As the driver rolled down his side window, diesel fumes from a succession of heavy old government trucks filled the air. The trucks, rumbling along at eighty kilometers an hour ahead of them, caused them to dodge about uneasily in their wake, trying to see the road clear to pass. The Security Major had taken out a nail clipper and now attended to a hangnail in a diligent workmanlike manner. Prisbek in the front seat wiped his neck, which was wet with sweat. Seizing an opportunity, the Colonel's truck, the Volvo and the station wagon at last darted out from behind the heavy government vehicles, overtaking at 120 kilometers an hour before pulling back in to the right-hand lane. Ahead was a long stretch of anonymous road, empty of all traffic.

He looked again at the Major, who had finished with the nail clipper and sat hunched in his seat, his arms folded across his chest, his brown straw hat tilted over his nose. The Major seemed to be staring at something on the floor and now, seeing that he was observed, said suddenly, "Where did you get those shoes, Eminence? They're Italian, aren't they?"

"Yes."

"I suppose you get a lot of your gear from Rome, do you?"

"Some things, yes." He put his hand in his jacket pocket and took out his zucchetto, showing the Major the little circle of red silk, then fitting the skullcap on the back of his head. "This, for instance. They don't make them here."

The Major flushed as though he had been insulted. "Take that off," he said, sharply. "Give it to me."

"Sorry. Why?"

"Give it to me! What's the trick? Trying to advertise that we have a cardinal in the car?" The Major snatched the little skullcap and, rolling down his window, pitched it into the breeze. "I don't know why a Catholic bishop would wear those Jew caps," he said. "You look like a sheeny rabbi."

"I am happy to look like a Jew."

"What are you trying to tell me?" the Major said. "Are you trying to tell me the Vatican likes Yids?"

"We are not supposed to hate anyone," he said. "I admit that in the past, our priests have been as anti-Semitic as the rest of our people. But we are trying to change that."

"Why bother?" the Major said. "Everybody knows what the Yids are like." He shifted in his seat. "Come to think of it, we made a mistake not searching you. What other little items of that sort have you hidden on you? Come on. Empty out your pockets."

"Sir!" the driver called. The Volvo braked, almost colliding with the Colonel's truck directly in front of it. Now, as they moved forward, the road ahead revealed a small queue of vehicles waiting at a road barrier. Soldiers with automatic weapons were examining papers. An armored weapons carrier sat in the center lane, a machine gunner in its turret.

"Damn," the Major said. "Give me the transmitter."

But as the driver reached into the glove compartment, the Major changed his mind. "Leave it. We're too close."

Their speed was now barely ten kilometers an hour. Ahead, the Colonel's truck came to a full stop, about thirty yards from the last vehicle in the queue. The Volvo also stopped. The Major got out and went ahead to confer. The station wagon, the third vehicle in their convoy, parked behind them. Its driver, the gray-haired man in the Security Policeman's raincoat, got out and came up to them.

"Vehicle check?" he asked the Volvo's driver.

"More than that, I think," the driver said.

At that point the Major turned and walked back to them. He seemed agitated. He went up to the driver of the station wagon and whispered something. The driver at once took off his Security

Policeman's raincoat and rolled it up. Under the raincoat he was wearing a red cardigan darned at the elbows. As he returned to his vehicle, he glanced in at the backseat of the Volvo, furtively, as though curious to see what the ecclesiastical prisoner looked like. Their eyes met and the man hurried on.

The queue of vehicles began to move up. The Major, seeing this, got back into the Volvo. "Well?" the driver said.

"It's all right. Go ahead," the Major said. He took off his straw hat and swiped his sleeve along the inside sweatband. He then turned and held out his hand. "Give me your ID, Eminence."

He hesitated, then reached in his jacket and took out his identity card. The Major looked at it: at the photograph, his name, Stephen Bem, the details of his height, weight, hair color, date and place of birth. "So your card's nothing special," he said. "And you have an ordinary name. Very common."

"God gave me a common name to remind me that I am nothing special," he said.

The Major handed back the card.

"Are they checking ID cards, then?" the driver asked.

"No. I think it's just a vehicle check," the Major said.

The queue of cars inched forward. As it did the Major touched the driver on the shoulder. "Move up one," he said. "We'll go first."

The driver obediently eased the Volvo out of the queue, moving it up in front of the Colonel's truck, settling into the space directly ahead. The occupants of the Volvo were now tense and silent. To his surprise he saw Prisbek, sitting in front of him, make a hurried sign of the cross and bow his head in prayer. Of course, why not? The Patriotic Clergy no doubt thought of themselves as God's servants and would ask God's help. But, in that instant, into his mind came the face of the driver of the station wagon, the one, who, minutes ago, removed his SP raincoat, revealing that he wore a red cardigan underneath. He knew that he had seen that man before and now he knew where. He was the man who walked up the aisle of the church in Ricany this afternoon, the one I thought was the priest. The one who went into the sacristy.

Prisbek, finishing his prayer, made the sign of the cross once more. Prisbek was not a member of the Patriotic Clergy: he was the opposite. He prayed now because he was afraid of being discovered by the soldiers. They were all afraid. They were impostors: the Security Colonel, the Security Major, all of them.

Ahead was a baker's van. The soldiers looked at the van's papers, then waved it on. The Volvo driver ground his gears and moved up, parking in the checkpoint area. A soldier came to the window. "Vehicle papers," he said. "And where are you going?"

"Moldova," the driver said.

The soldier took the papers, handed them to a sergeant, then peered inside the car. "Are you all together?" he asked. "Anyone getting a lift?"

He felt himself stiffen. "I am," he said. He reached for the car door and opened it, stepping out into the road.

"You didn't have to get out," the soldier said. "All right, show me your card."

He handed it over. The soldier barely glanced

at it before giving it back to him. "All right, you can get in again."

"No," he said. "I think I'll wait for another lift. I'm carsick." He turned back to the Volvo where the Major sat, holding the rear door open for him. He shut the door in the Major's face. "Go ahead," he said. "Thanks, but I need some air."

The Major at once rolled down the car window. "Get in."

"No, thanks. Thanks for the lift."

The soldier, impatient at this delay, suddenly rapped on the Volvo's roof. "Go on, move it up." A second soldier also rapped on the roof. The Volvo started up and moved through the checkpoint. The Colonel's truck now replaced it in the checkpoint area. He saw the Colonel and the man in Wellingtons staring at him from the front seat. "Vehicle papers," he heard a soldier say.

As the sergeant inspected the truck's papers, the station wagon bringing up the rear moved to the edge of the checkpoint area. He looked at the driver's silvery hair, at the red cardigan darned at the elbows. There was no mistake. He turned and scanned the countryside behind the road. Far up on the mountain slope was a small farmhouse. All around on either side of the checkpoint were open fields. As he stood there, watched by the Colonel and the man in Wellingtons, a soldier ran past, looking angry. The Volvo, ignoring the order to move on, had pulled in and parked a few yards ahead of the checkpoint. The soldier ran to the Volvo and hammered the butt of his automatic rifle on the roof. "On your way, on your way!" the soldier shouted. "You can't park there."

The Volvo drove off slowly and, as he watched

it disappear around a bend of the road, the Colonel's truck, cleared at the checkpoint, inched forward, coming level with him. The window was open on the Colonel's side. The truck stopped. "Want a lift?" the Colonel asked.

The Colonel's arms were folded across his chest. As the Colonel turned, from under his armpit the shiny barrel of an automatic pistol pointed directly at him. He looked back at the soldiers. They were busy with the station wagon, which had moved into the checkpoint.

"Don't be foolish," the Colonel said softly. "Just get in."

Obedient, he walked toward the pointing gun but, as he came closer, veered away, moving quickly out in front of the truck, walking across the road to the army weapons carrier that was parked in the middle divider. If the Colonel was a fanatic, he might risk everything. He might fire.

He reached the weapons carrier and stood, his back tensed for the Colonel's bullet. Knowing that he was out of earshot of the truck, he looked up at the machine gunner in his turret and asked quietly, "What time is it, please?"

"What's that you said?" the gunner asked.

"The time, please?"

"It's five-forty," the gunner said. The gunner pointed to the Colonel's truck. "You're holding up traffic over there."

"I'm not with them," he said, looking back at the truck, seeing the Colonel's face, drawn with strain, and the uneasy stare of the man in Wellingtons.

"You!" the gunner shouted suddenly, swiveling

his machine gun to point at the truck. "Move it!"

At that moment, the occupants of the truck seemed to panic. The man in Wellingtons put the truck in gear, reversed it and, turning, drove back through the checkpoint at high speed, going in the direction of Ricany. The soldiers at the checkpoint, surprised and startled, raised their automatic rifles as if to fire, but did not. He looked up at the gunner in his turret but the gunner had forgotten him. "They were cleared, weren't they?" the gunner shouted down to the soldiers.

"Cleared? Yes."

The gunner shrugged. The station wagon now drove slowly through the checkpoint and he saw a dreadful fear in the faces of the nun and driver. The driver hesitated, then drove on, disappearing around the same bend in the road as the Volvo, minutes earlier.

He turned away. Behind him were empty fields. He climbed down into the ditch and came up the other side, walking along a potato field, looking for a place to hide. If they came back down the road they must not see him. Halfway up the field there were deep furrows where potatoes had been dug. He looked at the road. The Volvo and the station wagon were coming back toward the checkpoint. He threw himself flat, burrowing down between the furrows as both vehicles parked on the roadside, about a hundred yards from the checkpoint. The Major got out, then Prisbek. They were joined by the driver of the station wagon and the man in the loden jacket.

He lay flat, peering down at them as they looked up, scanning the fields. Another car came through the checkpoint and as it drove past them, the Major ran out into the road, hastily scanning the faces of its occupants. Prisbek began to walk back to the checkpoint. The man in the loden jacket went into the field on the opposite side of the road.

He watched Prisbek. Prisbek would not dare to ask the soldiers if they had seen him take to the fields or if someone had picked him up. Prisbek was afraid of the soldiers. He watched Prisbek go to the checkpoint and loiter there, looking for him. Then Prisbek walked back the way he had come. The Major still stood in the roadway staring at each passing car. The man in the loden jacket had already returned to the station wagon and now was talking to the driver. The Major and Prisbek joined them and they all spoke briefly together. They then got into their vehicles and again drove to the checkpoint. Once again their papers were checked and they were waved on. He watched them drive back the way they had come, going toward Ricany.

12

Above him the sky whitened and seemed to crack. Seconds later, thunder rolled thickly across the empty fields. Rain burst from the clouds and when he stood up, his slicker sluiced water onto his trousers. The potato furrows between which he had lain had stained his kneecaps and hands, so that he now looked like a man who had been working in these fields. In the rain he walked down toward the road, moving well past the checkpoint. When he reached the road a heavy government diesel tanker was passing. It had switched on its lights and, as he tried to wave it down, a wash of dirty water from its tires splattered him, soaking his Italian shoes. The tanker went on. He waited until two further trucks had passed before venturing out onto the road again, and when he did he stood ready to duck into the ditch, should one of the Colonel's vehicles come searching for him. But now, he saw, approaching, a dilapidated old van, with, on its side, a crude painted sign showing two crossed knives. It was the sort of van owned by what his mother used to call traveling people, tinkers who sharpened knives and repaired metal pots, traveling from town to town, parking their vans at crossroads or in abandoned lots.

He did not think such gypsy people would stop for him and was surprised that the old van pulled up at once when he raised his hand to wave. The sliding panel door opened, revealing a traveling workshop of knife-sharpening equipment. In the front seat was a man in his thirties, a dark-skinned type with a snake tattooed on his right forearm. Beside him sat a blond girl, wearing a soiled silk dress and long ropes of imitation pearls. Both seemed drunk.

"Push over," the driver said to the girl. "Let him sit between us. Come on, dad. Hop up."

The girl stepped down to let him climb up beside the driver, then got in and pulled the sliding door shut. "Going to the city?" the driver asked.

"Yes."

"Do you have forty droschen?"

"Yes," he said. "And thank you for picking me up."

"It's for the gas," the driver said thickly. "The price of gas today, you can't pick people up for nothing. Would you have an extra ten droschen, by any chance? No, don't worry. Forty droschen's the price. But if you have an extra ten D's we'll all have a drink."

He took out his small fund and separated fifty droschen, which he handed to the driver. "Here you are," he said. "But I don't want a drink, thanks."

"You talk like a gentleman," the driver said. "He talks like a gent, doesn't he?"

"He *is* a gent," the girl said. "Look at his shoes. What line of work are you in, sir?"

"I'm a priest."

"Aha!" the driver said, and laughed. "Were you dodging the checkpoint, then?"

"Why would I dodge the checkpoint?"

"Because of what's going on."

"What *is* going on? I'm sorry, I don't understand."

"Let's have a little wet," the driver said. "Come on, Magda, I know you have another bottle someplace. Get it out. The gentleman paid for it."

"You've had enough," the girl said. "Any more and you'll have us all in the ditch."

"For Christ's sake," the driver said. "Want me to stop the van and give you a good belt?"

The girl shrugged, then pulled up her skirt, revealing her narrow thighs, black stockings and, between her legs, a bottle of slivovitz. She lifted the bottle out, letting her skirt stay up, smiling at him as she did. There was a certain sort of woman who took pleasure in seeking to embarrass or rouse a priest. He stared ahead at the road as she reached across him and took three plastic cups from a little ledge above the driver. "There, sir," she said, handing him a cup. "Hold steady."

He turned the cup, bottom up. "No, thank you." He looked at the driver. "Tell me. What *is* going on? Why was that checkpoint back there?"

The driver, now with a half cup of slivovitz in his hand, swallowed it in a gulp before answering. "We heard in Ricany that the army is setting up checkpoints on all the main roads. They're looking for stolen vehicles."

"Why?"

"They say somebody stole a lot of vehicles from a big government garage in the city, night before last."

"The Power is scared," the girl said.

"That's right," the driver said. "The Power is scared shitless. They say there's something big in the wind and the priests, they say the priests are behind it."

"The priests?" he said. "But why would priests steal cars?"

"Because of this big demo," the driver said. "But what am I telling you for? You're a priest, you must know all about it. There was priests handing out leaflets today in Ricany, about this demo next week. I mean—shit—they never did that before, not in the open. They're asking for real trouble."

He felt his mouth dry. "What leaflets?"

"Some shit about the national will and the martyrs of Rywald," the driver said. "I didn't pay it no heed."

"It said there's going to be some announcement on the twenty-seventh of August," the girl said. "That's Tuesday, isn't it?"

Suddenly the driver took a fit of coughing. The van careened across the road, almost running into the ditch. "Look out, Vlady," the girl called. "For Christ's sake, watch it."

"All right, all right." The driver pulled the wheel around, sending the van lurching back into the center of the roadway. "If it's a strike they're talking about, I can tell you it will never work," he said. "Never. The Power just brings up the water cannons and that's the end of it."

"Like the food riots last year," the girl said. "They put more meat in the shops for a couple of weeks and it all dies down."

"They'll shut our mouths with sausage, the way they always do."

"That leaflet," he said. "You said priests were handing it out?"

"No, it was kids were handing it out," the girl said. "But there was a priest with them. He had the handbills in a satchel."

"Where's the drink?" the driver asked, interrupting her. At that moment two cars traveling at high speed came up behind the van, flashing their lights. When he saw the cars in his rear mirror the driver hurriedly jerked the van off the road into the grassy shoulder. The cars went by, blue Ladas, unmarked. "The SP," the driver said. "Shit, man, I thought they were after *us*."

The speeding Security Police cars were already out of sight. The driver drunkenly slued the old van back onto the road as the girl, taking a hairbrush from her handbag, began to brush her long blond locks. He sat, no longer seeing the road ahead. How can it be that I knew nothing about this? Who has been keeping it from me? Kris Malik, Finder, Bishop Cihon, Monsignor Adamski—did no one on my staff know about those leaflets? Or do they know, some of them, and are they hoping it will happen? And what of Rome, what of the Nuncio? Has Monsignor Danesi heard nothing at all? Or is his trip to Rome a diplomatic absence? Is the Holy Father himself no longer my ally?

Ahead, a yellow light flashed at an intersection. As the van came up to it he saw that they were entering a suburb.

"Where are we?"

"Moldova," the driver said.

"We're not far from the city, then?"

"Half an hour, maybe a bit more. Depends on the traffic. Where will we drop you, Father?"

He turned to look at the driver. "Where are you going yourself?"

"We'll camp down under the river arches. We often sleep there."

Last evening, after the accident, he had stood in his quarters seeing himself in the mirror, his face bruised, his clothes torn. He had thought then that he looked like one of those drunkards who sleep under the arches of the Volya River. Tonight, he would join them.

13

At the intersection of New World Avenue and the Gallin Highway, the old van turned off down a winding side road that led to the Volya River. He did not know this road. It was a road of abandoned building sites, an empty lumberyard and several waste lots littered with rusting machinery, empty oil drums and, like filthy confetti on the ground, the discarded garbage of the derelicts who camped there. The van moved cautiously into one of these waste lots, the driver searching for a place to park. Abruptly, remembering his passenger, he braked to a standstill.

"This is it, sir," he said. "We sleep here. If you walk on down toward the river you can still catch a bus into town."

He thanked them and got down. In the darkness fires had been lit in the waste lot and as he walked back toward the road he saw people sitting around them, some drinking from pint bottles of vodka, others brewing tea in iron kettles placed among the hot coals. Ahead were the great stone arches of the Poniatov Bridge, the only bridge the Germans had failed to demolish when they fled the ruined city at the end of the last war. He walked on. The road ahead was lit by streetlamps that gave off an ugly blue light. There were no vehicles on the road, but as he went down toward the river people walked beside him, some trundling little handcarts on which were piled stocks of clothing, cooking utensils and bedding, others wheeling ancient bicycles, weighed down on either side with bundles of rags and bags of cast-off articles. There were few families among them. Most were men in groups of four or five, drunk and quarreling. Some walked unsteady and alone as though they went toward a prison. There were women, most of them old, or prematurely aged, as drunk as the men and equally quarrelsome.

Now he was directly under the great stone blocks of the bridge, and as he went into their shadows he saw many small fires along the embankment with people sitting or lying close to them, some already asleep. Here were a few children, wraithlike figures, wandering aimlessly among their elders. Under the bridge itself the stench of urine and vomit was overwhelming. He looked ahead at the great dark vein of the Volya River and across its dark chasm saw the lights of the Praha suburb on the farther bank.

He went on, coming out from under the bridge. He reached the edge of the embankment and saw, lying in the slime of the lower ramp, lapped by the river's fouled waters, a man and woman who seemed to be copulating. He turned back, looking up at the stone arches, at the span of the bridge and the traffic that crossed it high above him. It was, he thought, as though he had descended into a netherworld, unknown to those above. Ahead was a small fire, built by a low stone wall. Three men were there, men of his own age. He went to the wall and sat near the fire. No one spoke to him.

This is the underside of our state. And yet, I must remember that this misery is now less prevalent than in those days we speak of with false nostalgia. Maybe it's true, as that knife grinder said, that the regime stuffs our mouths with sausage to keep us quiet. But what of the other world, the world that Henry Krasnoy calls free? Are the poor any better off there?

He thought of the old days. They were not the days of freedom. They were the days when this country was run by and for Prince Rostropov and his friends. I told the bishops that. I said we must recognize that there has been much good in this social change. Of course, we want our freedom. But the West will not help us. The West has never helped us. We are alone.

He looked out at the darkness of the river. In the guttering flames of the small fire he smelled a stink of burning rubber tires. The man nearest him took out a fat roll of old newspapers and began stuffing paper between his jacket and shirt, as insulation. When he had finished he spread more paper on the stone parapet and lay down. Then, looking up at him, the man pointed to the remaining wads of newspaper. He said his thanks, stuffed paper in his clothing as he had seen the man do, then lay down by the fire. There in the stench of burning rubber, with a cold night wind coming off the river, he said his prayers and tried to sleep.

14

He woke to a bleary sky, streaked with the bloodshot rays of a rising sun. Above him, the great bridge and the sound of morning traffic. He rose, brushed off his clothing and walked along the embankment, past the twitching, snoring forms of his fellow sleepers, looking for the bus stop that the driver had spoken of last night. He found it at the junction of New World Avenue and a street called Redemption Boulevard and waited in line for the interurban bus to come. When he had paid for his ticket, he had just enough money to buy a roll from an old woman who came down the aisle carrying a tray from which she sold rolls and coffee to the early morning passengers.

The journey to Kollin on the outskirts of the capital took a little under an hour. When he alighted at Belnova Square an unusually large crowd of people was coming out of Santa Maria at the end of what he judged to be the seven-thirty mass. Was that a sign of the current unrest? He had noticed that, like a spiritual weather vane, church attendance swells in times of political confrontation. As he crossed the square, the church bell began to toll the hour of eight. He knew this church well: last Easter he had presided at a confirmation ceremony when three hundred children, dressed in white, took their vows as Christians. Yet, as the bell tolled the last stroke and he joined the new throng of worshipers crossing the square to attend the eight o'clock mass, again, for the second time in twenty-four hours, a church seemed not a sanctuary but a possible place of danger. And, as he came to the foot of the church steps, a blue Lada, emerged from a side street and cruised slowly across the square.

At the main entrance, putting out their cigarettes as though preparing to enter the church, were two men with the bored, unemployed look of raincoats on duty. Abruptly, he turned away. Had they seen him and would they now follow and arrest him? He walked quickly to the side street that led to the bus station and, after a minute, looked back. The raincoats were nowhere in sight. The blue Lada sat in traffic at the far end of the square, but then it was not unusual to see one in traffic. Am I, perhaps, imagining danger where none exists? If the SP did not listen in on Jan Ley's conversation with me, then Jan is waiting now in Santa Maria in the confessional, a safe place for us to speak.

Irresolute, he turned, walked a few paces in the direction of the church, then, uneasy, walked away once more. As he did, three schoolboys came into the square wearing the new red student caps favored by the regime. Each carried a canvas school satchel slung over his shoulder, but the satchels contained, not books, but leaflets. The boys advanced, holding out leaflets to any who would accept them. Several people did and he watched them as they stopped to read what was written. Were these the leaflets that had been passed out yesterday in Ricany? He began to walk toward the boys, looking around to see if any raincoats were in sight. Ahead of him, a woman carrying a large loaf of black bread reached for the leaflet offered by the nearest boy. He went up behind her. Perhaps she will throw it away and I could retrieve it later. If someone is observing the boys, it's prudent to wait. But the woman put the leaflet in her string bag and walked on. Now he was almost level with the schoolboy, who offered a leaflet for him to take.

"What is your school?" he asked, not accepting the leaflet.

The boy looked at him, uncertainly. "Santa Maria," the boy said. "Do you want one?"

He took the leaflet although he was certain that he was being watched. He glanced at it only long enough to read APPEAL TO THE NATIONAL CONSCIENCE in bold letters above a paragraph of smaller type.

Then, as though he disapproved of what it said, or was uninterested, he threw it away and walked on. He reached the northeast corner of the square, going toward Hanseatic Lane and the interurban bus station, and heard running footsteps behind him. He turned. Two raincoats were racing across the square in pursuit of one of the schoolboys. The other two schoolboys had been caught and were being held by plainclothes SP men. Three blue Ladas now stood at the exits to the square. A police whistle sounded. He walked on. He noticed that while one or two people had stopped to watch the arrests, most of the people in the square, like himself, went doggedly about their business as though nothing were happening.

"Sir?"

A voice, calling him. Behind him, a young man with a wispy blond mustache, wearing a dirty seersucker jacket and checked trousers. A hesitant smile and, in his hand, a leaflet. "Did you drop this, sir?"

"No," he said, staring at the smiling face. "I threw it away. What is it, anyway? I didn't read it."

"I didn't read it either, sir."

The leaflet, rejected, dropped from the young man's hand to flutter slowly and fall on the ground. Again, the police whistle sounded. He looked back at the square. The schoolboys were being bundled into the blue Ladas. The young man now stepped forward, as though to take hold of him. "Your Eminence," he said, in a whisper. "I have been asked to come and meet you."

"Who are you?" As he spoke, he noticed for the first time a tiny cross, sewn in white cotton thread on the young man's lapel. Younger priests who dressed in civilian clothes used these crosses as a badge of office. Yet it was no guarantee that its wearer was not an SP man.

"This is for you."

He took the cheap manila envelope that the young man held out. Inside was a thousand droschen in small notes and a scrap of paper. In Jan Ley's familiar italic hand he read:

Tonio.
To introduce Frederic Zaron, a former pupil.
Giannino.

He stared at the hesitant face. "Why did you hand me that leaflet?"

"It was your clothes, Your Eminence. I was looking for a priest. I couldn't be sure it was you until you turned around and I saw your face. Father Ley said it would be risky if you came to the church."

Who is he and why does he smile? Does he walk the corridors of Skoura Street, passing the interrogation rooms where people are tortured? Or is he from the Jesuit house? "You were a pupil of Father Ley?"

"Yes, Your Eminence."

"Tell me. In what year was Ignatius of Loyola born, and where?"

"In 1491 in Loyola Castle, near Azpeitia, Guipúzcoa, in Spain, Your Eminence."

"Thank you. How can I meet with Father Ley?"

"Have you had breakfast yet, Your Eminence?"

"No, not exactly."

"Father Ley suggested that you and I go to eat something in the coffee shop in Marshal Nilsk Street.

You will then go to the outpatient department in West Central Hospital. Father Ley goes there at nine-thirty, twice a week, for his dialysis treatment. As you know, it is a former religious hospital and the Nazarene nuns still work as nurses."

"Very well. We will walk to the coffee shop. It will pass the time. By the way, I think it better that the nuns not know who I am. I will simply say that I am someone Father Ley wishes to see privately."

"You will have no difficulty with that, Eminence. Father Ley often counsels people while he's undergoing dialysis. It takes four hours to change his body fluids."

They began to walk. He saw Zaron look around anxiously as they came out of Hanseatic Lane and went into Market Lane. He had accepted this young man's story, yet it could be a trap. Suddenly, he did not feel like talking anymore. This, he thought, is what life must be like for those who no longer trust each other.

15

In the coffee shop, when the waitress had brought the tray of morning rolls, Frederic Zaron leaned forward confidentially. "It's very simple, Eminence. You go into the main outpatient hall and go to the desk on your right. You will say that you came for the VD clinic and you will be given a number."

"Did you say VD?"

The young priest nodded, then giggled in embarrassment. "Yes, Eminence, I did. It's the venereal disease clinic on Sunday mornings. The dialysis patients are in rooms just off the VD clinic."

"So I will be given a number. And then?"

"They will ask who you wish to see and you will say Father Ley." The young priest looked at his watch. "I'd say you can go in any time now, Eminence." He rose. He had already paid for the coffee and rolls. "As you know, the hospital is just down the street."

"Aren't you coming with me?"

"Father Ley thinks it wiser for you to go on your own." He put out his hand, hesitantly, as though he were not sure that the gesture would be accepted. "Maybe we'll meet again in happier circumstances. Please, don't get up. I'll go now."

He shook the offered hand, which was damp and cold. He watched the young priest, or police spy, walk out of the large, crowded coffee shop. The music had changed and now he heard the familiar strains of "O Sole Mio." At once, he was back in Rome, walking along the banks of the Tiber with Jan Ley and a Dutch Jesuit called Klinghoffer, all three of them singing out of tune. How far away those days seemed, a happiness, a youth, he would never know again. He thought of Rome and asked himself: What will the Vatican say of these events? What will the Pope say? I cannot look to Rome—at least, not yet. I am alone here. The Tiber and the Volya are different rivers.

He stood up and, pulling the yellow slicker about his neck, went through the crowded café tables and out into Marshal Nilsk Street. As he walked toward the ugly concrete block façade of West Central Hospital, he realized the passersby were giving way, avoiding him, for, with his mud-stained trousers and ruined shoes, he now wore the disguise of failure, of those unhappy souls who begged in the streets for droschen to buy a morning vodka. At the hospital entrance he looked around for uniformed police, for raincoats, for blue Ladas or even for the young man, Frederic Zaron, lurking, waiting to watch his arrest. Two weeks ago after an episcopal conference meeting he had foolishly said to Kris Malik that he wished he were not always in the center of things. "How I would like to walk alone in the streets, unknown, to go home at night to an empty house, to the hidden solitary life." A wish granted is a wish destroyed. I am alone now: not hidden but in hiding.

As he walked through the hospital gates, there were no police or raincoats in sight. He sensed that Zaron had been telling the truth. In the main outpatient hall he went up to the reception desk. Behind the desk was a young woman in a white coat. She looked at him with no interest.

"I'm here for the VD clinic."

She took a plastic number tag from a pile. "You know where to go?"

"I'm sorry, no."

"Hall Two, on the left."

"Excuse me?"

Again she looked up, uninterested. "Yes?"

"I forgot to say I'm here to see Father Ley."

She gave a practiced sigh of annoyance. "Did I ask you who you were here to see?"

"No. Sorry. I just thought . . ."

"Take a seat. You'll be called when the time comes."

He went down the corridor, searching. Hall Two was a large room with terrazzo flooring and six long wooden benches facing a set of anonymous doors with frosted glass panels set in the wood. Perhaps thirty people waited on the benches, and when he sat down some of them looked at him, then looked away as though embarrassed to be seen in his company. At first this surprised him. Then he realized that they had long ago overcome their embarrassment at being here. Their distaste for him was, simply, because he looked like a derelict, a person who might be syphilitic, whereas they were, all of them, respectably dressed and showed no sign of their disease. Chatting to each other, they looked up occasionally when a young woman in a green smock appeared from the outer hall and called a number. He looked at his number. It was 17.

After a short time, the young woman appeared and instead of calling a number, turned and pointed at him. When he got up and went toward her she did not speak but led him, not toward one of the glass-paneled doors, but out into a corridor where she showed him a small green unmarked door. "In there," she said. "Doctor will be with you shortly."

He went in. It was a lavatory. There was a row of toilets and a row of washbasins and, hanging on hooks, several green operating-room garments. He stood there at a loss. A man wearing an operating gown and mask came in and went up to one of the washbasins, laying out on it a towel, which he opened to reveal a razor, shaving foam and soap.

"You need a shave, sir," he said. "If you please?"

In the washbasin mirror he faced a stranger, dirty-faced with a two-days' growth of beard. Lather foamed from the canister as he began to shave. His face stared back at him, unconfident, confirming his oldest fear; I am not fit to be a leader: the Holy Father, the college of cardinals, all have been mistaken in their judgment of my abilities. I have failed in my stewardship.

Behind him the man cleared his throat and gestured in impatience.

Hurriedly, he stroked his cheeks clean.

"I think if you leave your clothes here, sir, and put these on," the man said. "And what size shoe do you wear?"

"A nine."

When he had removed his soiled garments and put on the surgeon's gown and trousers, the man inspected him and, rummaging in a cupboard, handed him a gauze mask and a pair of rubber-soled shoes. "Try these shoes, sir."

They fitted. He laced them up and put on the surgical mask.

"And also this cap. Make sure it covers your hair. Now, if you'll follow me, please."

They went back down the corridor and passed through the hall in which the VD patients were sitting. This time the patients looked up at him and the other "doctor" with respect and interest. They went down a second corridor and came to a door. The man knocked briefly, then beckoned him to go in.

Jan Ley was in a hospital bed, his arm connected to a dialysis machine. He had removed his shoes and jacket and a large vein in his arm pulsed black and blue against his white, waxy skin as the machine silently did its work. "Sit down, won't you?" Jan said. "I think you can take your mask off, Doctor. I'm not contagious."

He pulled off the mask and suddenly, close to tears, bent down and kissed his old friend's brow. Jan's gray hair lay thin as a tracery on his skull. His eyes were dulled as if by drugs.

"How are you, Jan?" he said. "I'm sorry to get you mixed up in this."

"I've always been mixed up in your affairs," Jan said, with a smile. "Haven't I, Tonio?"

"Not like this."

Jan shrugged. He looked around at the bare institutional walls. "I'm told we're safe here," he said. "But there are two raincoats outside, sitting with the VD patients. They've been keeping an eye on me ever since your phone call yesterday."

"So we were overheard?"

"I believe so," Jan said. "About an hour after you called, two SP men came and took me down to Skoura Street."

"Oh, Jan, I'm sorry. Forgive me."

"No, no, they didn't beat me. They were polite. Still, it is a place of penitence, no doubt about it." Jan Ley looked at the dials on his dialysis machine. "I was interrogated by a VIP, General Vrona. You've heard of him?"

"Minister for Internal Security, isn't he?"

"And operating head of the SP, which is more impressive. Strange young man. Anyway, he seemed to know all about me. How long you and I have known each other, that I am your confessor, that sort of thing. I noticed they have computers in Skoura Street. Very up-to-date."

"What else did Vrona ask?"

"He wanted to know where you were. I said to him: 'You know very well where he is. You arrested him last night.' He said that wasn't true. He said you had disappeared of your own accord because you were plotting some action against the government. I said that was nonsense. He then asked me if I knew a man called Danekin."

"Danekin—the old prime minister? Lives in London now, doesn't he? Or did, the last I heard of him."

"Not *Anton* Danekin," Jan Ley said. "His son, Gregor. Gregor Danekin's body is in the morgue at Konev District Hospital. He's the one who tried to kill you. According to General Vrona, that is."

"Danekin." He saw again the bruised, bearded, arrogant face of the man who had tried to kill him. So that is why I thought of the old nobility.

"Did you know him, Stephen?"

"No."

"And his father?"

Anton Danekin, an aristocrat, filled with the prejudices of his class: anti-Semite, anti-Russian, but also anti-German. He had been deputy prime minister just before the war. A hero in the underground until the Russians arrived. "I never met him," he told Jan Ley. "I remember seeing him when I was a boy. He was riding in a state procession." A landau, on its way to parliament, surrounded by the elite National Hussars: Anton Danekin in the black dress uniform of the Hussars, gold facings, shako with red plume. "I was only ten then," he said. "Anyway, why would a son of Danekin's want to kill a cardinal?"

"This son, Gregor, was by Danekin's first wife,"

Jan Ley said. "He was educated here and became a teacher in an agricultural college near Ricany. And this is odd. He was a member of the Communist Party until eight years ago when he was expelled for drunkenness. After that he lived with his sister in a religious commune. Two years ago both of them dropped out of sight."

"How did you find that out?"

Jan Ley leaned back on his pillows. He seemed exhausted. "I told you," he said. "I have a little network of friends. The unions, you know. They're your friends too, Tonio. I think you need them."

"I need someone," he said. "I am alone. Tell me what else General Vrona said to you."

"I was coming to that. He gave me a message for you from the Prime Minister."

"From *Urban?*"

Jan Ley nodded. "Urban wants you to know that if you come forward now, the government will protect you. Of course, that's nonsense. They arrested you before, they'll arrest you again."

"They didn't arrest me, Jan."

"What? Finder said they did."

"The people who took me away the night before last were pretending to be SP men. It's part of their plan. Has there been anything in the foreign press about my being arrested?"

"Yes. It's international news, of course. There have been official protests from the British, American and French governments. And, of course, Rome."

"I was afraid of that."

"Why? What's going on, Stephen?"

"I'm not sure yet." Suddenly he felt severe pain behind his right eye. He bowed his head. "All of this is my fault. I should never have allowed things to go so far." He winced. Pain bore down like a dental drill. "The trouble is, I can't come forward now. The government won't arrest me, but they will watch my every movement. And if they do, I can't act to stop this."

Jan Ley leaned over and picked up his cigarettes. "Are we talking about a certain archbishop?"

"I think so. I know that the first thing I must do is talk with the union leaders. And I can't arrange that through my secretariat. That's why I've come to you."

"Yes, of course," Jan Ley said. "But why not through your secretariat?"

"Because, obviously, some members of my staff have lied to me about what's going on. Which means they no longer believe in my policies."

"Which union leaders do you want to see?"

"Jop. And it must be secret."

"Jop's in Gorodok. Would you go there?"

"Yes. I'll need a change of clothing. A train ticket, or a car, if someone can drive me. Is there someone . . ." But then he thought of Joseph. "No," he said. "I'll go by train."

As he spoke, a red light lit up in a socket above the dialysis machine. Jan Ley leaned forward and pressed the switch on a small box by his bedtable. "Yes?"

"Front desk calling Dr. Zaron. Dr. Zaron to front desk."

"Thank you," Jan Ley said and switched off the box. "Stephen, you've got to go at once. They told me if they made that announcement you must leave. Go, quickly."

He went to the bed and, bending down, embraced Jan. "Pray for me."

"I will. Now, hurry."

He went out of the room, pulling up his mask as he did. In the corridor a middle-aged nurse waited for him. "Dr. Zaron, this way, please," she said and led him not the way he had come but into a hall where he saw a sign. OUTPATIENT CLINICS. She hurried ahead of him and, as she did, he looked back. Two men in civilian clothes were entering Jan Ley's room. The nurse pushed open some swing doors. Above the doors was a sign. HEMATOLOGY–ONCOLOGY CLINIC. Inside in a small waiting area were six patients in hospital robes. "This way, Doctor," the nurse said. She opened a small side door and beckoned him to enter. He went in and she shut the door behind him. At first he could see nothing in the dark space, but then he realized he was in a closet, filled with brooms and cleaning materials. He could hear no noise outside. The migraine pain had ebbed, leaving him light-headed and nauseated. After a moment, feeling as though he might faint, he sat down on a drum of disinfectant. His eyes had become accustomed to the darkness. He thought of the days of his childhood when, after his father's sudden death, his mother had worked as a cleaner in Prince Rostropov's town house on Eastern Prospect Street while the Prince and his family summered at their country estate. There in the long hot afternoons he had roamed the corridors of the great empty house and, playing hide-and-seek with the caretaker's children, had hid in a closet with the caretaker's daughter, who kissed him and held her hand over his mouth, not wanting to be found. Now, in the dark, he thought briefly of that girl and into his mind came the bruised, bearded face of Danekin's son, the dying mouth opening to tell its secret, the words drowned in blood. Why did he try to kill me and who was that girl who drove the car? It doesn't make sense. It doesn't fit in with the plan of those who abducted me.

He prayed. O Lord, You have chosen me for this task. I have been blind to many things. My intellect is weak. I have not seen how many-sided is this world in which You have placed me in a position of trust. I am not fit to be a priest, let alone a prince of Your church, but I ask You to guide me now, to give me that strength and intelligence that I have failed to find in myself.

He was weeping. Shame at the memory of innocent schoolboys running across Belnova Square with leaflets provided by priests under his jurisdiction, schoolboys arrested by the SP for acts that, ultimately, were his responsibility.

He dried his eyes on his sleeve and tried to finish his prayer. Someone tapped on the closet door. A man's voice whispered. "Dr. Zaron, are you there?"

"Yes."

"In a few minutes we will bring some clothes. How tall are you?"

"Five feet eleven."

"Wait."

He waited. After several minutes, a large paper bag containing clothing was passed in to him. "I'll be outside," the man's voice said.

Inside the bag there was a shapeless turtleneck sweater that fitted him fairly well. The cotton trousers were, however, short in the legs. There was also a loose lightweight windbreaker that was too large and a battered old canvas hat. He emerged, pulling the hat down over his eyes. A young man was waiting, wearing a black plastic motorcycle helmet and the uniform of a government messenger. Over his shoulder was a large dispatch satchel. "This way, sir," he said.

They went out of the hematology clinic into the corridor, which was now crowded with nurses and technicians wheeling patients and trolleys of equipment in a scene of midmorning bustle. The helmeted messenger weaved through the confusion until they emerged in the main hall at the front entrance to the hospital. "Wait here, sir. I'll bring my bike around out front. When I come back in, just follow me out to the yard and get on the bike behind me. All right?"

He nodded. He looked about but the hall seemed innocent of surveillance. Awkward in his ill-fitting clothes he stood, shifting nervously, trying to avoid the eyes of passersby. He had never been sure how familiar his face was to the ordinary citizen, for although he had appeared frequently on State Television and had been photographed hundreds of times for newspapers and Church periodicals, he suspected that people saw, not the man, but the robes of office, the figure in crimson biretta moving in a Church procession or sitting in a bishop's chair at the side of the altar. Would anyone, seeing him in these nondescript clothes, imagine that he was the missing Cardinal Primate of this country?

Suddenly, hurrying through the revolving doors, the helmeted government messenger appeared, beckoned to him and, turning, went outside again. Who was he and how did Jan Ley know him? What was this network of people that Jan seemed able to summon up on a few minutes' notice? He began to walk to the entrance doors, looking to left and right to see if a raincoat lurked nearby. He went outside. At the curb, its engine coughing, was a small government motorcycle of the type he saw daily in the streets, noisy little machines, subject to frequent breakdowns. The messenger pulled down a black plastic visor, obscuring his features, and nodded to him to get on. He sat, clasping the messenger around the waist as they roared out of the courtyard and into Marshal Nilsk Street.

And now, wind in his face, dizzy as the bike swerved in and out of traffic, through Union Square, down New Street and across the Saxon Gardens into the old market area, where, twisting and turning, jerking to sudden stops to allow cattle to pass, the little bike at last spluttered to silence in a narrow old yard beside a large, mud-fouled refrigerator truck that was unloading pork carcasses. The young messenger pulled up his visor and waved to a man in a blood-splashed white coat who came forward as though he had been waiting.

He got off the pillion seat, his legs weak from the unaccustomed gyrations of the ride. The man in the butcher's coat touched his cap respectfully. "All right, Father," the man said. "We're just finishing up. When we do, you hop in the back of the truck, there. Smells a bit but there's blankets. Bundle up and you won't be cold."

The motorcycle messenger pulled down his black visor and turned to him, a faceless robot. "All right, sir?"

"Yes. Thank you."

"Father Ley said to tell you he'll try to get in touch with your party in Gorodok."

"Thank you. Thank you very much."

The messenger kicked down on the accelerator and his bike roared obedience. Six men were now crossing the yard, wearing heavy canvas cowls, carrying pork carcasses on their backs. The last man to pass waved to him and pointed to the rear of the refrigerator truck. He went over to it. A hand came down and pulled him up. Inside, it was icy cold. The man who had pulled him up came from the interior of the truck with several heavy, dirty blankets that he arranged in a nest on the floor. "Cold's turned off now," he said. "Better in a minute. I have to lock you in. Right?"

"Yes, fine," he said. "Thank you."

The man jumped down into the street. Heavy doors clanged shut and he heard a locking sound. Again, he was in darkness. He groped his way to the blankets and sat with them around his shoulders. The truck was filled with the sickly sweet smell of blood. After a few minutes he heard the cab door slam. The engines started up. Heavy gears engaged. The journey had begun.

16

"Did you sleep?"

The truck driver's head and shoulders were silhouetted suddenly in the theater of the opened truck doorway. After so many hours of darkness, of dreaming, of pain and discomfort from the jolting over rough roads, he stared dumbly at the man who asked the question. He smelled the freshness of the night air, saw the sky lit by the sheen of a full moon.

"Come, sir," the man said, and a hand reached up to help him jump down to the ground. Disdaining it, he jumped, staggered, but caught himself before he fell. His legs felt as if someone had kicked him in the kneecaps. "No, no," he said. "I'm all right. Thank you."

The man who had tried to help him was wearing one of the monklike butcher's cowls. He stood now like a medieval figure, waiting.

"Is this Gorodok?"

"Yes, sir. Do you know this place, sir?"

"I do, yes." He looked around and saw railroad sidings and, like mountains in the distance, the great moonlit slag heaps of the Gorodok mines. The refrigerator truck had pulled in front of what seemed to be a factory. A small light shone from a nearby watchman's hut at the factory gates, and now he saw the watchman, wearing his uniform, come out of the hut, carrying a lantern.

"Are you Mr. Zaron?" the watchman asked.

"Yes."

"Come down to the hut, then. I was told you might like a glass of tea and a bite to eat."

"Thank you."

The cowled butcher-driver turned to him suddenly, and awkward and affectionate, put his hand on his shoulder. "God bless, sir," he said and went around to the cab of his huge vehicle, climbing up, slamming the door. The heavy gears engaged and the truck moved out into the roadway.

"What time is it?" he asked the watchman.

"Eight o'clock, or thereabouts," the watchman said.

He looked down the road as the huge truck rumbled off under yellow fluorescent road lights. I was eight hours inside that darkness.

"This way, sir," the watchman said, shining his lantern to light the way, although the bright moonlight made it superfluous. They walked toward the small hut by the gates. Inside, on a fat-bellied iron stove, tea was brewed and at the watchman's tidy desk he saw hard-boiled eggs and a plate of ham. He had not eaten since breakfast and now he sat in the little circle of light by the window and hungrily fed himself. The watchman handed him a steaming glass of tea.

"What is this place?" he asked. "Is it a factory?"

"A factory, sir? No, sir, this is the old Borodin Mine. Number four. Closed now, of course."

The Borodin Mine. He could see, as on a television screen, banners and slogans, the massed miners kneeling in prayer in the main yard, the slag heaps in the distance, the line of soldiers, rifles ready, faces confused. He had been in Rome at the time, summoned for conference, and in the Spanish College had watched on a television screen that moment of the unions' greatest hope, the moment when it seemed, romantically, that the miners' will could nullify parameters of tanks and water cannons. Years ago; it was another age.

"Closed?" he asked. "Why is that, was it political?"

"No, no," the watchman said. "It's just that the mine's worked out." The watchman rose and went to the window as though searching for something outside. "There's talk now of making it a mine museum. Not stuff in glass cases, old helmets and lamps and such. No, they'll use the mine itself. Trips down the shaft. They'll show the pit ponies' stalls down below and the cages for the little sparrows they used to test for bad air. They'll show the tunnels. You know, sir, the men had to walk three miles to the pithead and their pay didn't start until they lifted a pick to hit the rock. The good old days. The capitalist times when a man worked ten hours a day for forty droschen a week. That's the talk, anyways, make it a museum. I hope it happens. If it does, I'm promised a job as a guide."

"You were a miner?"

"Yes, and my dad before me. That's the days I'm talking about, my dad's time. Ah!" The watchman peered more closely through the windowpane. "There's your lift, sir. You had enough tea?"

"Yes, thank you."

The watchman raised his lantern and waved it as if in signal. In the moonlight a small Fiat drove up and stopped in front of the gates. Its headlights flashed on and off. A young man got out of the car. He wore a red shirt and a blue plastic hard hat. He had left the engine running.

"Get along now, sir," the watchman said. "He won't want to hang about."

He went out into the moonlight. The young man was already in the driver's seat. He got in and they drove quickly down the road of yellow lights. "How was your journey, sir?" the young man asked.

"Bumpy."

"They didn't use the autoroute, then. No, I suppose they wouldn't."

They had reached an intersection. Ahead, beyond the traffic light, he saw a tangle of empty streets. He was not surprised. In the provinces few people went out after dark. From unlit windows there flickered the blue pools of television screens. The little Fiat now turned into an area of small gardens and backyards cluttered with clotheslines and coal sheds. The car stopped. "If you'll wait here, please?" the young man said.

He sat in the moonlight, watching as the young man opened a wooden gate and went down a long narrow garden allotment that was planted with tomatoes, lettuce and clusters of marigolds. It seemed a strange place to rendezvous. But then he remembered that Jop, at the time of his prominence, was always shown in pictures as a family man, a man of the workers, living a life of humble obscurity.

A dog barked and others took up the alarm until there was a loud discordant chorus. He saw the young man come hurrying back up the allotment path, his passing stirring the dogs to new bursts of noise. The young man opened the wooden gate and signaled to him to come. "Go straight down there, Father. You'll be met. Hurry!"

He half ran down the path: the cacophony of the dogs alarmed him. He expected back doors to open and the dogs' owners to appear. Ahead in the moonlight he saw a stout woman waiting on the path, her head tied up in a black kerchief in the old peasant style. She came to him, bowing in a manner that signaled she knew who he was. "This way, Your Reverence. This way!"

They entered a narrow cobblestone yard: ahead, an open doorway, lit from behind, the silhouette of a man, waiting. He went in through the door, blinded by the bright light of the kitchen. The waiting man was middle-aged and wore an old gray flannel shirt, moleskin trousers and heavy black boots. He was not Jop. Behind him, half curtsying, her face a mirror of respect, was a very old woman, her hand shaking in palsy as she beckoned him in. "This way, Your Eminence. Into the front room."

Cramped tiny rooms, an omnipresent smell of boiled cabbage: he knew these houses well. The front room, the parlor, was used only for visitors. He went in to face pictures of the Pope, the Virgin Mary, a man in a World War I private's uniform and, incongruously, a photograph of himself. And there, warming his backside at a small coal fire, was Jop. "Your Eminence," Jop said respectfully, but not deferentially. Unlike the others, Jop was accustomed to the presence of cardinals, Russian commanders, ministers, television crews. He came forward now, indicating one of the small armchairs upholstered in sickly green plush that were part of the furniture "suite."

He sat. At once, the stout woman, introduced now as "Mila, my wife," came in, nervous and anxious, awed by his presence in her house. "Can we offer you something, Your Eminence? Vodka or slivovitz? A glass of tea? I have prepared a little cold supper, nothing special, if you would honor us?"

"No, thank you." He smiled at her, practiced in refusing the hospitality that peasant people consider their first duty to a stranger who enters their house.

"Are you sure, Your Eminence?" asked the old woman, Jop's mother, who hovered in the doorway as though waiting his benediction.

"I have just had a very good supper, thank you, Mother," he said, smiling at her.

"But you must have something, Your Eminence," Jop's wife said.

"A glass of cold milk, then," he said. "That would be very nice."

He smiled at Jop, who waited with barely concealed impatience for these civilities to end. If a painter of the socialist realism school had been commissioned to paint a portrait of a loyal worker, he might have chosen Jop as model. His shoulders and massive forearms seemed fashioned to wield a pick or shovel. His monumental head was as noble as a Roman proconsular bust, sculpted gray curls, the jaw uplifted, skin pocked like stone with the badge of honor of his toil, the coal dust that years of pithead baths could not wash away. And yet, remembering Jop, the Jop of these past eight years, he knew that he was no longer a worker, nor ever again would be: he was now Jop the actor, doomed to play out his life's role as unofficial spokesman for the workers of this land, a man always waiting in the wings for the hot lights and the television cameras, the massed throngs, the cheers, the hands clutching at him as he passes through the packed union hall: a role not entirely different from that of a prelate in crimson silks.

"All right now, Mother," Jop said, dismissing her. He signaled to the man in moleskin trousers. "Mijal, you watch the door."

The parlor door shut. Suddenly, it was quiet in

the tiny room. Above the fireplace a cheap English alarm clock ticked loudly between two black-and-white china dogs. "You've been in the wars, Eminence," Jop said, smiling. "Now you know what it's like. Where did they take you? Skoura Street or the Citadel?"

"Then you don't know," he said. "It was not the SP who kidnapped me. Just the opposite."

"*Not* the SP? The foreign press said it was."

"Listen to me, Peter. I don't have time either to tell lies or to listen to them. Are you saying you don't know who kidnapped me?"

"On my word of honor, Your Eminence, I know nothing about it."

"All right, Peter, I believe you. But you do know about this 'demonstration of the national will' or whatever they're calling it. You're planning a total shutdown—factories, power stations, services—everything. Right?"

Jop turned away and stared at the small coal fire burning brightly in a fireplace of cheap green tiles. "I heard it was to be a one-day thing, a token shutdown, to show the Power what the people can do," he said. "But listen, Eminence, I'm not for it. The time is not right. I spoke against it at a meeting of the trades union council. The Power won't see it as a strike, I said. They'll see it as a challenge they can't back away from."

"You're right," he said. "And when is it to be?"

"This week, isn't it?" Jop said. "I hear it's set for Friday, three days after the celebration at Rywald. Someone's going to speak at the mass at Rywald. You must know about that, Eminence."

"I don't."

"Anyway it's not us who started this," Jop said. "It's the priests."

"What priests?"

"We were told the whole Church was behind it," Jop said. "Including you, Your Eminence."

He looked up. The parlor door was opening and Jop's wife came in with a glass of milk on a plate. "Thank you very much," he said, forcing himself to smile at her. He felt his hand shake as he took the glass.

Awkward, awed, she nodded and withdrew. "I was *not* behind it," he said. "That's why they kidnapped me. Peter, you said the time's not right. It's worse than that. If this happens it will be an act of national suicide. Haven't we learned anything in the past twenty years?"

"I said it's not my doing, Eminence. It's not the union style. We never forced the Power to choose between them and the Church. I was against this."

"Good. Then you must help me."

"It's not that easy, Eminence. Sorry."

"Why?"

Outside, in the night, the dogs began to bark again. Was someone coming? He saw Jop look at the clock, then turn to him, head bowed as if in confession. "It's this way, Eminence," Jop said. "We don't count anymore, the unions, I mean. We can't afford to speak out against the Church. Ever since the Borodin strike we have to try to show people that we won't let them down again. If the people want this demo and the Church is behind it, then we have to go along."

Jop clenched his hands convulsively, making them into fists as though he would hit someone.

He looked at those hands, at the nails blackened permanently by years at the pithead. "Peter, you are the leader of the unions," he said. "The men will listen to you."

"No," Jop said. "I'm in the same boat as you. I can't change the unions. They've made up their mind to go along. And maybe *you* can't change the Church."

"I *am* the Church," he said. "It will not happen. I promise you."

"I hope you're right, Eminence. Can I tell the others what you said?"

"Please. And now, I have to get to Gneisk. Tonight, if possible. Can you help me?"

"Transport? Of course. If you don't mind traveling in a truck, we can fix you up right away."

"Thank you. I know it's a risk for whoever takes me."

Jop went to the parlor door. "Mijal," he said. "Go and get Janik. Tell him we need the half-tonner. And the rest of you come in here. Cardinal Bem is going to give us his blessing."

They filed in, Jop's wife, his ancient mother, two teen-aged boys and another woman, who held a small child in her arms. They came, looking at him with that mixture of shyness and curiosity that he knew so well. But now he sensed their confusion. Could he really be that cardinal who, in his scarlet robes, smiled down at them from the photograph on the parlor wall? All knelt before him, including Jop. He made the sign of the cross and they made it also. He closed his eyes seeking, once again, to enter that place of silence where God waited, watched and judged. O Lord, we ask Your blessing. Grant us peace.

17

His new driver, introduced to him as Janik, was middle-aged and wore a leather aviator's cap of World War I vintage. He was taciturn. From the time they drove out of Jop's backyard until they reached the main highway fifteen minutes later, he was silent. Only as they approached a sign that read NORTH/SOUTH HIGHWAY did he turn and address his passenger.

"We're carrying a load of coal briquettes. If you're asked, we're delivering them to a government depot in Gneisk. I have an order sheet up there." He pointed to some papers affixed by a rubber band to the sun visor above the windshield. "Look in the glove compartment. You'll find a temporary ID card. It's out of date, but that doesn't matter. If you lose your permanent card, the stupids at the ID office issue these for a month. But everyone knows it takes six months to get a new one."

He reached in the glove compartment and found a worn, dirty temporary identity card. It stated that his name was Stanislaus Wick, that his age was forty-six and that he was five feet six inches tall with brown hair and blue eyes. Like his clothes, his new identity did not fit him. "This fellow's a lot smaller than I am," he remarked to the driver.

"Doesn't matter. They never look. That's why we're carrying briquettes. People think if you have briquettes on a truck this size you're not going to any government depot. So when the police stop us, it's to nick a few briquettes for themselves. Briquettes are hard to find, even in the coal region."

"What about the army? It seems to me, they're the ones making road checks."

"The army's looking for stolen vehicles. And guns. You don't have a gun, do you?"

"No, no."

"Then you're all right. Music bother you?"

He shook his head. Music, as loud as in an organ loft, flooded the cab of the truck. In its meaningless mix of rhythms his thoughts ran on a treadmill of unpleasant hypotheses. He remembered the time when half a million Warsaw Pact troops had been massed on the frontier after a report, fabricated by the Soviets, announced that counter-revolutionary groups had turned to open confrontation with the government. It could happen again. Except that this report would not be fabricated. The leaflets are real. Could it be that the Russians might use this incident to get rid of the present government and install one even more amenable to Moscow rule? And if so, is it my duty to prevent that?

He was tired. The music, the ribbon of road ahead white and lonely in the headlights, acted like hypnosis to lull him to sleep. He woke, after what must have been an hour, to find the truck passing through a village, its streets empty, houses dark. They halted at a traffic light and he looked at the shuttered storefronts of a small plaza, at a solitary cat running like a thief across the road to disappear into an alley. The light changed to green. As the truck went on he saw, at the other end of the village, a flashing red light and two vehicles parked in the street. He turned to the driver. "What is it?"

"Don't know. It's the wrong time of night," the driver said, enigmatically.

They drove on. As they did the flashing red light changed to a fixed red light. A uniformed policeman stood beside the light, holding an automatic rifle. The truck stopped. At once, three policemen gathered around. One shone a flashlight on the load of briquettes. A moment later someone climbed on the tailgate of the truck. The driver, Janik, turned to him and winked. "I told you," he said.

Suddenly, a bright light flashed into the cab, blinding him.

"ID," a voice said.

He handed down the temporary card. Janik handed his card to a policeman on the other side of the truck. After a short interval the cards were handed back. "Got an order sheet for those briquettes?" a voice asked. Janik took the papers down from the sun visor. There was a pause. "Scarnia Depot," a voice said. "All right, we're going to take you in."

"What?" Janik's voice was loud, surprised, aggrieved.

"We have orders to check on all deliveries. We'll have to phone Scarnia Depot to see if this lot's all right."

"But it's the middle of the night," Janik said.

"Well, we'll have to wait till morning, then," the voice said. "Move over."

Suddenly, the cab door was opened on his side and a uniformed policeman climbed in beside him. "All right," the policeman said to Janik. "Just go straight and take the first turning to the left."

Janik put the truck in gear. "I don't give a sod about these briquettes," Janik said. "I'm not going to spend the night in the police station because of a load of fucking briquettes. You want the briquettes, you can have them. I'll dump them off at the station, if you like."

The policeman did not answer. The truck turned left. "Straight on down the street," the policeman said. "Now, turn in here. That's it."

The truck's headlights showed a yard where a police car was parked. There were also two other cars. "I'm not joking," Janik said. "I'll even unload them for you."

The policeman ignored this. "All right, both of you come with me. And give me the ignition keys."

It was many years since he had been in a police station. As a young priest he had sometimes gone there to arbitrate a family fight, or try to have a drunken parishioner released with a caution. But now, as he entered the main room of this police station, the policeman marched them straight to a sort of cage at the rear of the room. Inside, several men and women were sleeping on bunks while others stood or paced the concrete floor amid a stench of vodka and vomit. "Wait a minute, what's all this?" Janik protested. "We didn't do anything, did we?"

The policeman unlocked the steel-barred door. "There's beds in there. It's a good six or seven hours before we can phone the depot, right? In you go."

The door swung shut. The policeman turned a key in the lock. At the desk in the main room was another policeman slumped, asleep, his head pillowed on his forearms. On the wall behind this policeman was a notice board with photographs of missing persons and criminals wanted by the police. One poster was larger than the others and prominently displayed. It was different in that it bore no written message. It was simply a reproduction of a photograph and under it was scrawled WATCH FOR . . . The face in the photograph was his.

He turned away as though his photograph face had recognized him and might call out, announcing his identity. Agitated, he went up to Janik, who had lit a cigarette and also stood staring through the bars. "Look," he said. "Above the one who's asleep." Janik looked, then blew two funnels of smoke through his nostrils. "Well, then," Janik said. "I'd get into bed, if I was you."

He went to the row of bunks and, avoiding a snoring man in a lower bunk, climbed up onto the upper one and lay on a hard pallet that smelled of sweat. He turned his face to the wall. *If only I am not recognized there is a chance that tomorrow morning they will let us go. But are the briquettes black market, or are they really scheduled for that depot at Scarnia? I must ask Janik.*

But it was too dangerous to get out of the bunk. If a passing policeman recognized him, or if one of these drunken and unfortunate people looked at the photograph and then at his face? *If I am held here I cannot stop Krasnoy, I cannot prevent the worst from happening.*

He felt the heavy sickness of despair. The words of St. Paul came into his mind. *Who has known the mind of the Lord, or who has been His counselor? How*

unsearchable are His judgments, how inscrutable His ways.
If it is His will that I be recognized and held, who
am I to question that will? All that I can do, all that
I must do, now, is pray.

He prayed. As he did, some poor wretch vom-
ited nearby and another called out curses in his sleep.
To suffer contumely in Jesus' name, wasn't that what
I once wished for?

A voice called out a name. The cell door opened.
A policeman entered and went up to Janik.

"Asleep," Janik said. "Over there."

A hand tugged on his shoulder. "Come on. Get
down."

The policeman led them out into the main room
of the police station, where, standing by the desk,
there were two young men wearing blue jeans and
imitation-leather windbreakers. One, who was very
tall, chewed a matchstick, which he licked to the
corner of his mouth before speaking. "Which one of
you is Janik Stryka?"

Janik raised two fingers in a mock salute.

"You're Peter Jop's brother-in-law, right?"

"Proud of it," Janik said.

The tall young man turned to the policeman
who had stopped them at the roadblock. "We were
following them in a car but our fucking car broke
down," he said. "That's why we phoned ahead to
get you to hold them. Have you checked their truck?"

"Yes. Just coal briquettes," the policeman said.

The tall one then turned back to Janik. "So
you're going to Gneisk. In the middle of the night."
He pointed. "Who's this one?"

Facing him while the SP man spoke was his
photograph, head and shoulders in a cassock and

cape. The SP men stood with their backs to this photograph. "ID," the tall one said.

He handed over the temporary card. The tall one looked at it, then looked at him. "Grown a bit, haven't you?" He turned to the other SP man. "Search him."

The other young man came up, his hands quickly patting hips, buttocks, chest, then pulling open the loose jacket. "Empty out!" the young man shouted. "Get your fucking crap on the floor. Quick!"

He had no belongings save his own identity card, his ring and the money. He pulled out the ring and the money and dropped them on the floor. "That all?" the tall one asked.

"Yes."

At that, the other one began pulling at his pockets, turning them inside out. The real identity card was brought out and handed to the tall man.

"More like it," the tall one said, studying it. He looked at it again, then looked up, his eyes excited as though he had won a lottery. "Bem. *Cardinal* Bem!"

The uniformed policeman and the two SP men now circled him as though he were some strange animal. The second SP man looked up at the wall and ripped the poster from its place on the board. Like an actor playing in pantomime, he danced forward bearishly and held the poster photograph over his head. "Looky here, looky here," he chanted. The tall SP man stared up at the photograph with wild affection and uttered a yell that echoed eerily in the room. "Jesus fucking Christ! Oh, pardon me, Your Eminence." He turned to the second SP man. "Boychik, thank God for your lousy carpool Fiat. If it hadn't gone on the blink, we'd have followed them all the way to Gneisk and let them be picked up by the Gneisk squad. And we wouldn't have got any fucking credit!"

"*I* was the one who stopped them for you," the uniformed policeman said.

"Fucking right, you were. I'll see you get a mention. Now, get some chain on both of them. Where's the red phone?"

"In there." The uniformed policeman pointed to a side room. Again, the tall SP man gave his eerie howl. "Come on, boychik. Let's tell the Major."

The uniformed policeman now came up with sets of chains. Both he and Janik were first handcuffed, then their hands were shackled to a long chain leading to their ankles, which were similarly shackled. As the policeman fitted the ankle chains he looked up. "I'm sorry about this, Your Eminence. I'm a good Catholic. It's just my job."

"That's all right," he said.

Apologetically, holding them by their chains as though they were dogs on a leash, the policeman led them to a bench beside the toilets. They sat, shackled, facing the large prisoners' room, the inhabitants of which came crowding to the bars to stare at them.

"I got you into a bad mess," he said to Janik.

"Not to worry, Eminence. I'm used to being a guest of the government. Where will they take us, do you think?"

"I don't know."

At that moment the tall SP man came out of the side room followed by his partner. They went up to the desk, grinning. "VIP service," the tall one said to the uniformed policeman at the desk. "Where's Mito airport?"

"It's a military base, about ten miles from here," the policeman said.

"All right, we'll need two cars. One for us and another car as escort."

"We only have two cars," the policeman said. "And one's out on patrol."

"Get on the horn then, and call it in. Let's go!"

18

An hour later, passing under a lamp above the door of a military Quonset hut, he and Janik, awkward in their chains, were led out along a tarmac path to a waiting two-engine aircraft. The SP men accompanying them now seemed nervous. Closer to the aircraft he saw two men standing by a passenger ladder. One wore the uniform of a lieutenant general of the army, with gray-green tabs that identified him as a member of the general staff. The second man, much younger, was dressed in a dark suit, with a gleamingly white shirt and a red woolen tie. His hair lay flat on his skull as though it were a coat of shiny black varnish. His pale pear-shaped face, with large unfocused eyes, seemed less like a human face than a child's unfinished drawing. It was this strange person who at once riveted the SP men to attention. "Who put those chains on?" he asked, in a voice strangled with rage. "Get those chains off His Eminence, at once!"

The tall SP man knelt down on the tarmac like a pilgrim about to receive a blessing. His fingers fumbled with the key to the leg chains. The uniformed general, a heavily built man with a head of gray hair thick as a terrier's coat, came up and bowed slightly. "I am General Kor," he said. "You may remember our meeting in Prague, when I was on Minister Scarzynski's staff."

"I'm afraid I don't. And I would be obliged if you would also remove my friend's chains."

The General turned uncertainly to the man in the dark suit. "This is a matter for Internal Security, I think," he said. "So, it's up to you."

The strange young man now came up close. "From our point of view, Your Eminence," he said, in his strangled whisper, "security on the aircraft would be better assured if Mr. Jop's brother-in-law were at least handcuffed. So, if you don't mind. . . ."

"But I do mind," he said. "If he is to be handcuffed, then I shall be handcuffed too."

The strange young man's eyes at last seemed to focus on him for an instant. Then he snapped his fingers. At once the SP men went to Janik and removed his chains.

"As you can see, we wish to extend you every courtesy, Your Eminence. We apologize for the chains. I assure you these men will be reprimanded. Now, if you will come this way. . . ." He pointed to the passenger ladder. "And mind your head as you enter the aircraft."

He went up the ladder and into the plane, which was a military aircraft, bare of furnishings. An air-force sergeant came to help him with his seat belt. The strange young man settled in on his left, the uniformed general on his right. Minutes later they were airborne, the Mito airport a tiny oasis of light in the darkness below.

The strange young man leaned toward him offering a cigarette, raising his voice to be heard over the noise of the engines. "The journey is only half an hour, Your Eminence."

He refused the cigarette. "You are from the SP?"

"Yes."

"And what is your name?"

"It doesn't really matter, Eminence. I'm merely your escort."

"What is your name?"

"Vrona."

"So, you are the Minister for Internal Security. *General* Vrona?"

The man held up his hands, palms outward, as if in surrender. "Yes," he said. "But these military titles seem odd, when, as you know, we are policemen, not soldiers."

"But you kill people."

"The courts order death," said the strangled voice. "Not the police. Our interest is peace and order within the country."

General Kor leaned forward. "Did you say something, Eminence?"

"No. Nothing."

Vrona, putting a hand on his knee, as though to quiet him, said, "It's difficult to talk in this noise, Your Eminence. Save your breath, Eminence. There will be plenty of talking ahead."

The sky outside lightened to a predawn pallor. A few minutes later they came down, buffeting through clouds to circle the Volya River and land on a runway, far distant from those used by international aircraft on commercial flights. They were expected. He saw a light truck approaching, towing a portable stairway. Waiting on the tarmac were two blue Ladas and, behind them, coming up a support road, a long black Zis limousine, its headlights blazing. When the aircraft door opened, General Vrona went ahead of him, obsequious as a butler, cautioning him to mind his step as he came out into the cold dawn air. Far down the tarmac, soldiers with automatic rifles were stationed at fifty-yard intervals and, as the uniformed general led him to the Zis limousine, a captain appeared, saluting. "General Kor, sir?"

"Yes, what is it?"

"It has been suggested that the prisoner travel in a Security Police vehicle, two vehicles behind this limousine. As a security measure, sir."

"His Eminence is not a prisoner," the uniformed general said, crossly. "But yes, very well, where is the vehicle?"

And so he was led to one of the cars he knew so well but had never traveled in before, an anonymous blue Lada. When he got into the backseat Vrona was already sitting there. Vrona leaned forward, scanning the road ahead as the Lada moved out, two cars behind the limousine. The soldiers lining the tarmac turned away from the approaching cavalcade, watching in the dawn shadows as though an enemy lurked along the lonely runways.

"Why so much security?" he asked.

"Because of the assassination attempt the other night," Vrona said. "Of course, you know all about that. I have a transcript of your conversation with the doctors at Konev Hospital. Did you know the assassin personally, Your Eminence?"

"I saw him only for a moment before he died. He was not someone I knew. I believe he was drunk."

"Yes," Vrona said. "He was a drunkard. It would seem he was not acting on anyone's orders. We believe he was acting on his own. Would you agree?"

"I told you. I know nothing about him."

"A pity," Vrona said. "It was probably foolish of me, but for a moment I had hoped you would enlighten me."

"Where are you taking me?"

"You have not yet had breakfast," Vrona said. "That shall be our first concern."

They were now entering the outskirts of the capital. Government trucks were the only heavy traffic abroad at this hour. They passed people on bicycles and motor scooters and, from time to time, the long rubber-tired farm carts like coffins on wheels that still brought produce in to the central market from outlying farms and collectives. Soon, he saw that they were skirting the center and coming in by Motowska Bridge, a route that led them through the northern suburbs and onto the Boulevard Lenin, which had been Konigsberg Boulevard in the old days. At the end of the boulevard, their colors made golden by a reddening morning sky, the curiously Russian domes of the old Mallinek Palace.

At that moment the Zis limousine, the escort cars and an army vehicle that preceded the others split off and turned down Proclamation Avenue. Their little blue Lada went on alone, coming up to the main gates of the palace, where a police guard stepped out of his sentry box and casually waved them on. Lonely in that great driveway left over from a more formal time, the little car turned left at what he recognized as the side entrance leading to the Prime Minister's private quarters. This driveway was graveled, and loose chippings of stone rattled against the Lada's undercarriage as it drew up under a porte cochere. The SP man in the front seat at once jumped out, drawing his revolver and peering around. But there was no one in sight in the Prime Minister's garden, save for a soldier half concealed behind a laurel bush facing the doorway. At the door a servant waited, an old man who in former days might have been a butler. He wore a steward's gray jacket and gray cotton gloves and bowed respectfully as they passed through into the entrance hall.

Floors of white Carrara marble, marble busts of princes, marshals and medieval kings, gave the hall a funereal appearance. Their footsteps loud on the uncarpeted marble staircase, they followed the old servant up to a first-floor landing where two uniformed soldiers of the tank corps stood with automatic rifles in a formal position of ease before a heavy walnut-paneled door. There was also, on this landing, an SP man with a walkie-talkie and, high in a balcony behind a marble bust of a long-dead prince, a third soldier looked down, his automatic rifle trained on the visitors. The walkie-talkie crackled unintelligibly. The soldiers came to attention. The SP man pushed open the heavy paneled door and

Vrona gestured for him to go in. He entered into a gloomy hallway, curtained against the morning light. Behind him the paneled door closed. He was alone. He stood, his eyes trying to penetrate the gloom, when, suddenly, a door opened ahead of him and a silhouette appeared in it. A familiar voice said: "Stephen. Good morning."

He went forward. The Prime Minister's private quarters looked at first glance to have been furnished like the library of a gentleman's club. A black-and-white spotted Dalmatian dog came up to him, nuzzling his hand, then moving away, having approved him as a visitor. He saw, beyond the library room, a second room where a handsome mahogany table sat in a window recess and on it a silver coffee service, pots of jam, honey and the traditional morning rolls.

"Come in, come in," said the familiar voice. "We are alone. Well, in a manner of speaking. I have long ago stopped worrying about such things."

The morning light from the window recess shone on the Prime Minister's face. The Prime Minister was wearing an old military sweater with black leather elbow patches and a strip of black leather along the shoulders; his trousers were khaki corduroys and his shoes and shirt were of similar military hue. He seemed taller this morning, as he stood by the breakfast table. When they had met before, the Prime Minister had always been seated, or surrounded by a cluster of aides and guards. This morning, he did not look military, but professorial, his balding head laureled with a wreath of sandy hair. His spectacles were old-fashioned, with heavy black frames and lenses behind which his eyes seemed large, floating and vague.

His body was the body of a soldier, strong, but thickened by age. He has changed, as I have. We are older. For the Prime Minister was a contemporary in more ways than one. They had both attended the same Jesuit school. They each had won the senior Latin prize, one year apart.

Now, as they sat down at the table in the window recess, the handsome Dalmatian dog flopped down at the Prime Minister's feet. The Prime Minister, General Francis Urban, seemed at home in this former palace and indeed, looking at Urban, he remembered that he had been known at school as one of the richer boys, son of a landed proprietor, descendant of a distinguished military family. It was natural for an Urban to become a general, even to become prime minister. What was not natural was his route to this power.

"Coffee?" Urban asked, holding up a silver pot. "You look tired."

"Black, thank you," he said. "And yes, I am a little tired."

"Hungry?" The Prime Minister offered a basket of hot morning rolls.

At that moment he saw himself in the gilt-framed mirror that rose from floor to ceiling at the end of the table: a nondescript figure in cast-off clothing. As though the same thought had occurred to the Prime Minister, Urban said, "Tell me, Stephen, what's happened to you? Why are you dressed like a tramp?"

"It's a long story," he said. "And confusing."

"Tell it to me."

"I can't. I'm not sure that I know it myself."

"Stephen," the Prime Minister said, "let me ask

you a question. Do you not think it a grievous sin for men of God to act like terrorists?"

"What do you mean?"

The Prime Minister rose and went into his study, returning with a folder of large black-and-white photographs that he passed across the table. They showed what seemed to be an explosion at some public building.

"Did you know about this, Stephen?"

"About what?"

"Those are the military barracks in the Praha district. Yesterday, someone put a thousand-pound bomb in the dormitories. By what I suppose *you* would call a miracle, there were only minor injuries when it went off."

He looked at the photographs again. Suddenly, he felt sick. "Why did you say 'men of God'?"

"Because an hour after this happened we intercepted a clandestine broadcast from somewhere in Gneisk Province. A group calling themselves the Christian Fighters is claiming responsibility. And the broadcast ended with the words, 'Come to the mass at Rywald. Remember the Blessed Martyrs.' "

"The Christian Fighters? Who are they?"

"Who?" The Prime Minister's eyes shifted suddenly behind his thick-lensed spectacles as though trying to detect some hidden deceit. "I believe they are the same people who kidnapped you."

Prisbek, the Major, the Colonel, the strange nun. He looked at Urban and said, slowly, "Perhaps. But why did they try to pass themselves off as the Security Police?"

"Don't you know?" Urban said, an edge of anger in his voice. "It was a plot to take you out of circulation and make the outside world think we'd done it."

"But why?"

"Why? You must know why! Stop these Jesuit tricks, Stephen. I have no time for lies!"

"I am not as well informed as you are," he said. "I still ask you, why would they lay the blame on the SP?"

"Because, if you were arrested by the SP, people would think that *you* were behind this plot. As, indeed, you may be."

"I know nothing of any plot. No one has confided in me, not even my own staff."

"Really?" Urban said. "So you're the innocent party? Then why, when you escaped from those people you thought were Security Police, did you not go back to your residence? Why did you go secretly to see Jop? Who brought you to Gorodok? Why are you wearing those clothes and why were you in a coal truck last night with Jop's brother-in-law, driving to Gneisk? That is not the behavior of an innocent person. What about these leaflets your priests are putting out calling for some sort of national demonstration? Do you want a confrontation with us and our larger neighbor? Years ago you came to me and asked me to help make an agreement between Church and State. I helped you make that agreement. I risked my political life, then, remember that! I did it to avoid further strife. I did it for the national good."

The national good. He stared at this man, at the flushed face, the angry eyes behind thick lenses. In his years in power, Urban had survived strikes, food riots and a change in party leadership, always with that phrase on his lips. The national good. For Urban, there was no difference between the nation and the State. It was not the national good, but the preservation of the State, that he served. It was true he had made possible the concordat between Church and government that permitted the Church to have a say in its own affairs. It was also true that the promises made in that agreement had been consistently broken. But this was not the time to bring it up. "I don't want civil strife any more than you do," he said. "You must know that."

"Then what about this?" The Prime Minister held up the photograph of the ruined building, his hand trembling in anger. "Do you realize the game your priests are playing now? Flirting with terrorists? Do you want this country to become like the West—terrorists blowing up airports, assassinating people? You know we won't stand for it—to say nothing of the reaction of our larger neighbor. Right-wing terrorists in East-bloc countries. And backed by the Church!"

"That is nonsense," he said. "The Church will never back terrorism."

"Then what about these leaflets?"

"These things were done without my knowledge. I was trying to put a stop to them. That is why I went to see Jop."

"Is *he* behind it?"

"No. But the unions will have to support demonstrations, if they occur."

"Then who *is* behind it?" Urban said. "I will tell you what I think. The Christian Fighters is a terrorist group financed by the West—probably by the CIA."

"Possibly," he said. "But no small terrorist group could marshal the forces needed for a national demonstration of protest."

"Quite! And who *has* the power to shut down the country, Your Eminence? You have! Which is why this is happening on the eve of the religious celebrations at Rywald."

"That is true," he said. "And every minute I sit here talking to you is a minute wasted, if I am to put a stop to it."

The Prime Minister leaned down and fondled the Dalmatian's neck. After a long moment, he looked up and said, "For once, I think—I want to think—that we are on the same side. Tell me who *you* believe is behind this. It might help my decision as to whether or not I should let you go."

"First of all, you have no right to detain me. Secondly, we will never be on the same side. Years ago you went to the Soviet Union as a prisoner, arrested after a student demonstration. Five years later you were a Soviet officer in a crack military school. You, whose ancestors fought for this country's independence. It sickens me to hear you talk of the national good. You know your regime is hated and feared by most of your countrymen."

"You don't understand patriotism as I do," the Prime Minister said. "Remember, no matter what you think of me, I am trying to hold this country together. And only I can do it. I am willing to accept that I am disliked."

"You are trying to hold this country together as a satellite of a foreign power. Therefore you are not a patriot, but an agent of that power."

"And Rome?" the Prime Minister said. "Isn't

Rome a foreign power? Isn't your true allegiance to Rome and, ultimately, to the West?"

"I do not trust the West any more than you do. We both know that for the West this country is a pawn in a larger game. The West does not care about us and will not help us."

"Well, to Rome, then," the Prime Minister said, irritably.

"My orders do not come from Rome!"

As he said these words he realized that he was shouting. I am unfit to be a leader. Why did I lose my temper? Why did I speak as though I hate him? "I apologize, Francis. I should not have insulted you. I love this country and I am sure that, in your own way, you love it too. Perhaps you are right. For once, we have the same objective. Give me twenty-four hours. Do not have me followed. I will see what I can do."

The Prime Minister bent down again and fondled his dog, scratching it behind the ears. The Dalmatian's tail clumped on the marble floor as dog and man looked into each other's eyes. Then the Prime Minister said, "I know the man you are going to see."

"Do you? Then you must also know that my time is short."

The Prime Minister did not speak. He sat studying the cups and plates on the breakfast table as though they were pieces on a chessboard. At last, he said, "I cannot promise that you will not be followed. But those who follow you will be discreet."

"There must be no arrests."

"I cannot promise that. If we must, we will act. I will give you twenty-four hours. How will you travel?"

"May I have a car? And for my driver I would like the man who was with me last night."

The Prime Minister rose, went into his study and picked up a telephone. "Vrona, will you come in, please?"

He heard the outer doors open. The Dalmatian growled, its ears pricked. "Down!" the Prime Minister cried, taking hold of the dog's collar. A moment later the inner door opened. The Dalmatian barked and strained forward. Vrona's slicked-down hair shone in the morning sun as he came in, keeping a wary eye on the dog.

"I suppose you're aware of what's been said?" the Prime Minister asked. Vrona hesitated, almost shyly, then nodded and smiled.

"Well, can you arrange it as the Cardinal wishes?"

"Of course, sir. But may I ask if we can really afford twenty-four hours?"

"Vrona," the Prime Minister said. "For centuries the Roman Catholic Church has thrived on arrests and persecution. With each arrest of a priest we strengthen the position of those who are the enemies of the government and of the Party. I do not say that I trust Cardinal Bem. But I know that certain forces within his church have tried to deceive him. Therefore he must still have the power to alter the course of these events."

"But *will* he alter them?" Vrona asked, turning, with his strange flirtatious smile, as though to deny the insult of his words. "I mean nothing personal, but in my view, His Eminence is a sworn enemy of socialism, an agent of the West and a fomenter of unrest. There is no way in which I will ever believe otherwise."

"I am not interested in your beliefs, Vrona," the Prime Minister said. "I am telling you that I have decided to give Cardinal Bem twenty-four hours. After that we will do what we must do."

"With respect, sir," Vrona said. "I would suggest that we do not wait any longer. Act now! We have proof enough."

The Prime Minister turned from Vrona. "We are talking about martial law, Your Eminence. If I impose it, I will not lift it in a week or in a month. We will act to defend the State. If there is any demonstration, stoppage, strike or whatever, I will send troops against the demonstrators. There will be arrests, detentions, interrogations such as this country has not seen before. I will do this because I intend to show that we can continue to run our affairs without outside assistance. Now, it's up to you." He turned to the SP chief. "Vrona, will you please get the car and driver? His Eminence has not much time."

Vrona left the room. The Prime Minister went to his desk and opened a drawer. "Here," he said. "You may need some money for your journey." He took out a stack of clean bills, saying, "Just let me count this." But he did not count the bills. Instead, he wrote something on the white band surrounding them. When he finished, he handed the bills over, saying, "There, that should be enough. A gift from State to Church."

He looked at the note written on the band in Urban's small neat handwriting.

If you need me, phone 4708000.
It is a safe number. A message
there will reach me.

As he put the money in his pocket the outer doors opened and Vrona came through into the Prime Minister's study. "The car is ready," he said. "And your driver is on his way. Will you come downstairs, Eminence?"

The Prime Minister's Dalmatian suddenly began to bark at Vrona. "Down, down!" the Prime Minister cried, running to hold the dog. "Good-bye, Cardinal Bem."

19

In the cool of the morning, a mist rising over the city obscured the sun, dulling the golden sheen of the palace's domes above him. He stood in the porte cochere at the entrance to the Prime Minister's apartments, watched by the uniformed police guards, the armed soldier, the palace butler and, pacing up and down, the obsequious yet intimidating figure of General Vrona. After a few minutes he saw, approaching up the long central avenue, the black Zis limousine that earlier had met him at the airport. Behind it was a police Lada.

When the Zis drew in at the porte cochere, Janik got out of the backseat and came up to him, smiling. "I hear you want your driver, Eminence."

"Yes, Janik, if you don't mind," he said. He noticed that the police Lada had stopped behind the limousine and now its driver came to Vrona with the car keys. "You'll take the police car," Vrona said, pointing to the Lada. "We'll send the limousine on ahead with two men in it, in case someone is looking out for you. You're going to Gneisk, I assume?"

He looked at Vrona.

"Well, *aren't* you?" Vrona said. "You may as well tell us. After all, we have to follow you. For your own protection, of course."

He did not answer. He saw Vrona hand the car keys to Janik and again caught sight of himself, this time in the mirrored reflection from the gleaming black side panel of the limousine. And as he saw that stranger in a stranger's clothing, he realized that in the last hour all the rules had changed. He was no longer a man on the run from the police and hidden enemies. There was no longer time to practice any sort of caution. From this moment on, he must draw danger toward him. "No," he said. "We are not going to Gneisk. I have changed my mind. Will you give Janik the keys to this limousine?"

"Are you insane?" Vrona said. "This is a car that draws attention. It is not in our interest to see you killed. Believe me, you need our protection."

"In that case," he said, "I will be happy to accept a police escort. But I will travel in this limousine."

"But where are you going?" Vrona asked. "An escort to where?"

"To Lazienca Street," he said.

"You are not going to Gneisk?"

"No."

"If we escort you back to your residence, it will look as though you have been detained by us and are now being released."

"You do not have to escort me," he said. "But I assure you that the moment I return to my residence I intend to make a public announcement saying that I was not detained by the government."

"May we have that in writing, Your Eminence?"

"You do not need a written statement," he said. "You have my word." As he spoke he got into the backseat of the limousine and signaled Janik to join him. The limousine door shut. Looking through the window he saw Vrona raise his hand in signal and at once the motorcycle police kicked down on their starters. The Zis moved out into the central avenue and went through the main gates into the city streets. Before it and behind it were police Ladas filled with armed SP men. Weaving motorcycle police raced ahead, blocking traffic at intersections as the cavalcade approached in a procession reminiscent of the progress of a head of state. It went down Proclamation Avenue and entered Proclamation Square, driving over the same cobblestones where, three nights ago, Joseph had been killed.

From now on, I must draw the danger toward me. As always, I am Your servant. Do with me what You will.

20

Servants and staff stared at the Zis limousine parked in the courtyard of the Residence; faces came up to him, voices, questions, as he hurried toward the elevator to his private quarters; telephone ringing, he, naked in the shower, calling out instructions to Kris Malik in the adjoining study. Later, with Tomas acting as his dresser, he robed himself in the uniform of his calling: cassock, crimson silk sash, zucchetto, pectoral cross. In the triptych mirrors he saw again that other person, symbol of the Church and its authority, as Tomas, stooping, picked up the cast-off clothes he had discarded.

"What will I do with these, Your Eminence?"

"Wait." He went to the jacket and, inside, found the bank notes given him by the Prime Minister. He tore off the wrapper with Urban's private number, then handed the bank notes to Finder. "Take this and put it in the fund for religious instruction."

"Eminence." It was Kris Malik, coming from the telephones in the study. "I've just talked to State Television. They say you may make a taped broadcast, not a live one. They cannot permit a live broadcast without knowing in advance what is to be said."

"I have no objection to a taped broadcast," he said. "But the crew must come here, to the Residence. What about the head of the secretariat?"

"Monsignor Grabski? He's on his way, sir."

"And Father Ley?"

"We have sent a car for him, Your Eminence."

He turned to Finder, who waited with memos of telephone calls that had been received in his absence. "Was a requiem mass said for Joseph?"

"Yes, Your Eminence, in the cathedral. Monsignor Jelen officiated."

"Good. Kris, please telephone the Residence of Archbishop Krasnoy and see if you can get him on the line."

He saw Kris Malik hesitate. Can it be—no, it can't be that Kris is among those opposed to me.

"I'm sorry, Eminence," Kris said. "I haven't had time to explain. When it was announced on Saturday that you had been detained by the government, the episcopal conference called a meeting here for this afternoon. Archbishop Krasnoy is probably on his way from Gneisk at this very moment."

So God has guided me, after all. I did not go to Gneisk. "How many of the bishops will attend?"

"Seven, Eminence. Bishop Ziemski is ill."

"None of the bishops know that I have returned?"

"No, Eminence, not yet."

"Good. Let us keep it that way. Father Finder?"

"Eminence?"

"When the bishops arrive I want them to be taken to the main drawing room, as usual. But do *not* say that I have returned. They will be coming in when—around two o'clock?"

"Yes, Eminence. The meeting is at two."

"What if the servants or staff tell them?" Kris Malik said. "Or if the government announces that you have returned—surely it's in the government's interest to say you are safe and that they did not abduct you."

"Yes, you're right," he said. He held out the torn money wrapper. "Call this number and say I would like to speak with the Prime Minister on a matter of urgency. Do it at once. And Finder. When Father Ley comes, send him to me."

"Yes, Your Eminence." Finder held up his sheaf of memos. "What about these calls and messages?"

"Later. You may go now."

He watched Finder depart, then went to the

door of his study. Kris Malik was on the telephone. "Yes, the Cardinal . . . Yes, we'll hold on."

"Kris?" he said, then hesitated. What can I say to Kris? He has always been loyal to me. There is no reason to suspect him.

"Eminence?" Kris held out the receiver.

He waited for the familiar voice. "Cardinal Bem?"

"Prime Minister. There will be a meeting of our bishops at two o'clock this afternoon. I would be grateful if you would delay announcement of my return until, say, two-thirty. I do not wish the bishops to know in advance that I am here."

"I hear that you have asked for television time," the Prime Minister said. "I hope you are not planning some trick."

"The speech will be taped. As you know, Prime Minister, you, not I, control the media."

"Very well. We will delay the announcement. But rumors spread fast, you know."

"I know. Thank you, Prime Minister."

He put the telephone down. As he did, Tomas came from his bedroom, holding Bashar by the collar. The big dog strained toward him, wild with joy. "He missed you, Your Eminence," Tomas said. "You and Joseph. He's been sitting moping ever since you disappeared."

"Let him go, then," he said, and the dog, released, jumped up on him, undisciplined as a puppy. He thought of that other dog, the Dalmatian, gazing into its master's eyes. Urban is unmarried: they say he lives an ascetic life. We have this in common: a dog at the foot of our beds. "There boy, there boy," he said, wrestling with Bashar. Tomas handed him a biscuit, which he fed to the dog, then stood up, brushing off his cassock. "Kris," he said. "What about those leaflets that appeared this weekend?"

"Yes, we've seen them. Apparently they were distributed here and in Gallin and Gneisk provinces."

"By whom? Who authorized it?"

"We've been told by some parish priests that they were authorized by Bishop Charnowski and Archbishop Krasnoy."

"Have you asked Krasnoy and Charnowski about this?"

"Monsignor Grabski did. Both bishops denied knowing anything about it."

"Do you believe them, Kris?"

"I don't know what to believe, Eminence. We did find out that the leaflets were printed here in the city."

"Where?"

"By an underground press in the Praha district. It's called CF. Last year they printed some poems by Lork and at the time of the food riots they printed a leaflet calling for a people's uprising."

"CF?"

"Christian Fighters, Eminence. It's a small group but Monsignor Grabski believes it has links with Washington."

"How does he know that?"

Kris smiled. "I don't think he does, Eminence. Sometimes, as you know, the Monsignor confuses hypotheses with facts."

"Kris," he said. "Please. If you are not on my side, now is the time to say it."

"What do you mean, Eminence?"

"Do you think I am a careerist, in league with the government?"

"Eminence, how can you ask me that?"

"Just a moment. If the Church could bring this country to a token standstill, by some sort of national demonstration, would we be able to win concessions from the government?"

He saw his secretary hesitate. "It's only a guess, Eminence, but I think it's possible. I think the Russians will allow General Urban to settle this in his own way."

"You said 'will,' Kris. Is that my answer? Are you part of this?"

"No, Eminence," Kris said. "How could you think that?"

"I'm sorry." He put his hand on Malik's shoulder. "But who *am* I to believe? How can these things have happened without my knowledge?"

"Eminence." It was Finder at the doorway. "Father Ley is here. Will I send him up?"

He turned from Kris and looked at Finder. Was Finder to be trusted? Suddenly, he felt ashamed. Of course I must trust him. *As you would that men should do to you, do you also to them in like manner.*

"No," he said. "I'll go down."

In the main hallway he saw Jan Ley, a small frail figure, wrapped in a woolen scarf, although the day was warm. He went to him and embraced him. "Giannino."

"Tonio. What is happening?"

But, at that moment, two of the secretariat priests, walking up and down the hall conversing, lingered, covertly watching them. "Come, Giannino," he said, and led Jan into a small room, the same room in which he had talked with Joseph's wife the night Joseph was killed. Again, he was confronted with the large painted statue of Jesus that stood just inside the doorway and, again, the statue's hand, raised in the traditional gesture of blessing, seemed to warn him to be careful of what he said.

"What *is* happening?" Jan asked again as soon as the door was closed. "There are police and SP men thick as a swarm of bees around this place."

"I am the object of government protection."

"I am glad to hear it," Jan said. "You know, don't you, that by coming back you have put yourself at great risk?"

"Have you heard about the barracks that was blown up in Praha yesterday?"

"Oh, my God," Jan said. "Then, it's true. They *are* planning terrorist acts."

"Who? Henry Krasnoy?"

"I don't think so. Whoever's behind this is more dangerous than Krasnoy."

"Have you heard of a group called the Christian Fighters?"

He saw Jan stare up at the painted statue as though the statue had said something. "Eminence," Jan said, slowly. "Who mentioned the Christian Fighters?"

"The Prime Minister. This morning. He also told me about the Praha bombing."

"Oh, my God," Jan Ley said again. He went to the table and sat on one of the chairs that surrounded it. "Yes, it's possible."

"But who are they?"

"Do you remember Waldemar Keller?"

"I never met him," he said. "Didn't he put out a clandestine magazine for the Catholic intelligentsia? It was published in London, wasn't it? I think he denounced our concordat with the government."

"Yes. He lived in London. His uncle was Prince Radors-Keller, remember—the old National Front?"

"You said *lived* in London. Is he here now?"

Jan Ley shrugged. "If the Praha barracks was bombed, I suspect he is."

"Then there *is* a connection with the leaflets?"

"What do you mean, Tonio?"

"They were printed by an underground press here. The press is called CF. Christian Fighters."

Someone knocked on the door. "Yes?"

It was Finder. "The people from State Television have arrived, Eminence. Where shall I put them?"

"What did we do last time?"

"We filmed in your study, Eminence."

"All right. Take them there."

But, in the end, it was decided that he should be filmed on a balcony of the Residence with a clear view of the city behind him.

"So that people can see that you have returned and that there is no deception," said the director of State Television. "Will that be all right, Your Eminence?"

"Yes, of course."

He had written some words on a sheet of paper and now he quickly memorized them. As the cameras focused on him, one of the television people spoke into a portable microphone. "Stephen Cardinal Bem, interviewed at his residence on Lazienca Street today."

The director nodded for him to begin. Looking into the eye of the camera he became uneasy, as though he already saw himself on television, heard himself speak as though the words had been dictated to him.

"My beloved people. In the last few days a mistaken report was issued saying that I was detained by the government. I wish to state categorically that this statement was untrue. I was, at no time, detained by the government. I left my residence and went to a place of repose to prepare myself for tomorrow's Jubilee celebrations at Rywald. I will attend those celebrations wherein we honor the bicentenary of the Blessed Martyrs. I bless you all."

The director came forward. "Excuse me, Your Eminence, but you stumbled a little there in the middle. Would you like to do it again?"

"No," he said. "Thank you very much. This will not be broadcast until this evening. Correct?"

"Yes, Eminence. It will be on the evening news."

When the television people left, he remained on the balcony, looking down into the central courtyard. Two cars were parked there and others began to arrive. He saw the familiar figures get out, greeting each other, formal but friendly, like tribal chieftains meeting on neutral ground. Some of these bishops were younger than he but most were of his generation. He saw John Charnowski, tall, with a flayed, pitted face, his left side trembling: Parkinson's disease. He was one of the two bishops who might have authorized distribution of the leaflets. He saw Charnowski look around the courtyard, then go to Bishop Kott, drawing him aside. The other bishops, talking among each other, were now being led toward the main hall by Finder. And then, as he watched them go in, a last car drove into the courtyard. It was a huge old American Buick, ungainly among the smaller European vehicles. The driver jumped down and opened the rear door. Archbishop Krasnoy descended, looking around the yard, then turned to stare up at the windows of the Residence.

Quickly he stepped back, concealing himself in the shelter of his apartment.

The palace drawing room in which the bishops' conferences were customarily held was large and dark with gilded formal chairs and, on its walls, oil portraits of bishops and cardinals who now looked down on their successors. As he approached the doorway he saw that the bishops had not yet seated themselves and that servants were passing around glasses of tea and small sweet cakes. He went in quickly. "Brothers," he said. "Welcome."

Faces turned to him. The room was stilled by the shock of his presence. Some came up to him at once, as though to comfort him. Hands held his, voices spoke in a jumble of greetings. Smiling, nodding, he looked beyond, to Henry Krasnoy, who, across the room, turned and looked at John Charnowski, exchanging a glance that confirmed his fears.

"Brothers," he said. "Please be seated."

He waited as the gilded chairs were pulled up to the long conference table. "This meeting was called, I am told, because of my absence. God be thanked I have returned and am well. I was not taken prisoner by the government as has been alleged. I was held by another group. Do any of you know who this group could be?"

There was a silence.

He continued. "What is important is that, during my absence, leaflets have been circulated asking for a national demonstration next Friday, three days after the Jubilee celebrations at Rywald. It has come to my attention that this leaflet has been written in a way that implies the Church's collusion in such a demonstration. I ask you now. Does anyone know who wrote this leaflet?"

Again, there was a silence. Old Bishop Kott said, at last, "Damned if I know. It was not distributed in my diocese."

"Not in mine," Bishop Wior said. "Nor mine," other voices said.

"Then where was it distributed?" he asked.

"In Gallin," John Charnowski said.

"And in Gneisk," Henry Krasnoy said.

"And in my own diocese," he said. "I saw it distributed by schoolboys of the Santa Maria school. And those schoolboys were later arrested by the SP. I ask you now. Where did those leaflets originate? I am told they were printed here in the city."

Monsignor Grabski, the head of the secretariat, now spoke. "Your Eminence, it is true that they were printed and distributed here and in other places in this diocese. I have been trying to find out who authorized it, but I am sorry to say there is some confusion in this matter."

"And who in *your* diocese authorized their distribution?" he asked, turning to Bishop Charnowski.

The pitted face looked up at him, cold and defiant. "I did, Your Eminence."

"And in yours?" he asked Henry Krasnoy.

"I wrote the leaflet," Krasnoy said.

At once there was a hubbub around the table, a

murmuring that he stopped by raising his hands. "Thank you, brothers," he said. "I wish to say now that I disavow the sentiments expressed in this leaflet. There will be no demonstration of any kind against the government as a result of the Rywald celebrations tomorrow. The Rywald celebrations are to honor God and the Blessed Martyrs, who will, we pray, one day be canonized as saints. The Church, as you know, has great power in this nation. That power is given to us by God. It is given for the purpose of saving people's souls, not for political thrills. I do not have to remind you of this, brothers. There may be other episcopal matters that you wish to discuss since you have come so far for this meeting. But now, if you will excuse me, and if you will excuse Archbishop Krasnoy and Bishop Charnowski, I would like to see both of these bishops in my apartment. Thank you."

He rose, gave his blessing and left. In the corridor he waited with his back to the open door of the conference room until he heard someone come out. He turned around. Henry Krasnoy, his florid face impassive, stood facing him. Behind, holding his shaking arm tight against his chest, John Charnowski. "If you will come this way," he said. "There is an elevator."

In the small Swiss elevator, which had been put in some years ago when his predecessor suffered a stroke, he brought them up to his apartment. No one spoke until he had opened the door to his study and shown them in. Bashar, dozing on his blanket, looked up, then hid his nose between his paws. John Charnowski went to the window, looked down, then turned around. "Why are there so many police outside?" he said. "Is it true that someone tried to kill you? Is it to be believed?"

"Yes."

"How did he try to kill you?"

"He?" He looked at Charnowski. "Did you know the man?"

"Of course not," Charnowski said, angrily. "We were told this story by that secretary of yours, Father Malik."

"I'm sorry," he said. "I'm afraid I've become overly suspicious, these past days. Forgive me, John. You asked about this man. I am told he is Anton Danekin's son."

Again, he saw the two exchange a glance, quick as a scissor's closing. "Danekin, yes," John Charnowski said. "He was a leader in the underground during the war—a great patriot."

"Perhaps. But it was his son, Gregor."

"Why?"

"I may be mistaken, but I think he may have considered me an obstacle to whatever plan you gentlemen have in mind."

Krasnoy's florid face darkened as if filled with an angry flow of blood. "What are you talking about, Your Eminence? Are you implying that we would try to have you killed? Are you mad?"

"I hope not," he said. "And again, I apologize for my suspicions if they are unfounded. But you have identified yourself today, Henry, as the author of that leaflet. The leaflet was printed by a group called the Christian Fighters. Danekin was a member of the Christian Fighters."

"Who told you that?" Krasnoy said in a loud, bullying tone.

"No one. It is a supposition. I do know that his sister, who drove the car that night, is a member of that group."

"What?" Charnowski, his arm shaking with palsy, turned to Krasnoy. "Henry, what's going on?"

"I had nothing to do with it," Krasnoy said. "Yes, I knew Danekin. I know the family. Gregor, the son, was a Communist at one time and a drunkard. He and his sister are fanatics, both of them. If he tried to kill you he was acting on his own—entirely against orders!"

There was a silence in the room. "Against whose orders?"

No one answered.

"Your orders, Henry?"

"Of course not. I am not a member of the Christian Fighters."

"But you know them?"

Krasnoy did not reply. Bishop Charnowski cleared his throat. "Yes, we know them. They are a patriotic group, a Catholic group who are dissatisfied with present Church policies."

"In what way are they dissatisfied?"

"Well . . ." Charnowski hesitated. "They don't believe in cooperating with the government, as you do."

"Collaborating!" Krasnoy said in his loud aggressive voice. "Collaborating with those whose aim is to destroy our faith and enslave our country."

He looked at Krasnoy for a long moment. "Do you realize what you are saying? I am the Primate of this country with authority invested in me by the Pope. You have insulted my position and you have defied my wishes. Do you want that sin on your conscience? Do you?"

Krasnoy looked quickly at Bishop Charnowski, who looked away as though he did not wish to speak to him. Seeing this, Krasnoy walked to the window and stood there, his back to both of them. He looked down into the courtyard as he spoke. "I realize the gravity of what I am doing, Your Eminence. But I am acting according to the dictates of my conscience. Certain forces have been set in movement and it is too late to stop them. Frankly, I do not wish to stop them. It is my belief, and I think it is also Bishop Charnowski's opinion, that in this country the Church does not at present have the leadership it deserves."

"Leadership, Henry? What sort of leadership did you have in mind?"

"I am talking of the new Church leadership in other countries. In South America, for instance. You know what I mean."

"I do not. It is my understanding that you, personally, disapprove of the present Church leadership in South America. In any event, we are not a South American country, but a country in the Soviet bloc. There is no possibility of an extreme solution here. We *can* win further concessions from the government. We can force them to take steps to ameliorate the conditions under which our people live. But only if we act responsibly, and at the proper time. That is the Holy Father's position, as you well know."

"But this *is* the proper time," Krasnoy said. "The country is behind us."

"Behind who? The unions do not want this demonstration. They did not instigate it. You started it, didn't you? And you don't know a damned thing about running a strike or negotiating with the government. Henry, I am asking you. Don't force me to take this up with Rome!"

"I am not forcing you to do anything, Your Eminence. You must do what you think is right. And so must I. And now, if you will excuse me, I will return to Gneisk to complete the preparations for tomorrow's celebrations."

"Wait," he said. "That address you were writing, the one you were planning for tomorrow. I told you to tear it up and write another one. Have you done so?"

Krasnoy did not answer.

"I will be in Rywald tomorrow," he said. "After the mass *I* will deliver the address. Not you. Is that clear?"

"I am the Bishop of Gneisk," Krasnoy said. "Rywald is in my diocese."

"*I* am the *Cardinal*," he said. "We will not discuss it further."

"If you will excuse me, then," Krasnoy said. He walked to the door, and paused. "John, can I give you a lift?"

Bishop Charnowski, holding his trembling arm close to his side, looked at him, then said, "No, thank you. I have my own car."

"Then I will see you tomorrow at Rywald."

The door shut. Bishop Charnowski said, "May I sit down, Your Eminence? My damned leg is hurting."

"Of course, John. Sit here."

Stiffly, Charnowski sat on the leather settee, facing the desk piled with papers. His head began to tremble incessantly as though he had lost control of his movements. "Henry told me . . . he said the

Christian Fighters had taken you away for a few days to prevent you stopping what we hoped for. I didn't know anything about this other thing. I'd never be a party to harming you. . . ."

"What *did* you hope for, John? Tell me."

The old man's shaking head stilled for a moment as he burst into speech. "A demonstration of the national will. A great shout of No!"

"John, answer me. Do you think the Holy Father wants this country to become a battlefield?"

"I don't know what Rome wants anymore," the old man said. "Where is the Pope this week? Brazil? Japan? Who knows?"

"Yesterday a military barracks was blown up. By the Christian Fighters."

"What barracks?" The old man's head began to shake again.

"In Praha."

"But he said, maybe a strike, a sit-down. . . ."

"Who . . . John, who?"

"Keller," the old man said. "Waldemar Keller."

"Is he the head of the Christian Fighters?"

Charnowski bowed his head and sat for a moment as if stunned. "If he bombed a military barracks . . . then he lied to us. . . . I must speak with him. I must speak with him now."

"Take me with you, John."

"I can't. You are surrounded by the SP. They will follow you."

"Where is he? Is he in the city?"

Charnowski's head again began to tremble.

"John, answer me."

"He is in Rywald, waiting for us. I will be there by evening. I will speak to him."

"Then tell him this. If there are further terrorist acts I will urge our people to denounce those who perpetrate them. Furthermore I will refuse the sacraments of our religion and excommunicate those who support them."

The old man, head shaking, stared at him, without speaking.

"John?" he said. "Will you tell him, John?"

Slowly, in the slate-colored eyes which stared at him, he saw tears form, tears that the old man's tremor made spill out onto his cheeks. "Yes, Your Eminence. And forgive me."

21

At eight o'clock that night he said mass in the chapel of the Residence. When he had finished, he knelt again in front of the altar, in the long shadows of a late summer evening. He was still on his knees when Finder came to him, excited, to say that he had just watched him speaking on the evening news.

He rose and left the chapel. As he came through the long corridors of the episcopal offices, he could hear phones ringing, and when he reached his apartment, Kris Malik, Monsignor Grabski and Tomas were there. "There have been several calls," Kris said. "The foreign press, American television, some of the Western embassies. What shall I do, Eminence? Whom do you wish to speak to first?"

"No one. Monsignor Grabski, will you tell the press that I will give no interviews? Say that I am preparing the sermon I shall deliver tomorrow at the Rywald celebrations."

"And the embassies, Eminence?"

"Tell them the same thing. I have no time. Remember, I want to leave early for Rywald."

"Yes, Eminence."

"Kris, do you remember that part of the address Archbishop Krasnoy intended to give at tomorrow's mass? You brought it to me the night of the accident."

"Yes, sir. I think—let me look in my files."

"Tomas," he said. "Will you please pack my robes for tomorrow's ceremonies? Has Bashar been fed?"

"Yes, Your Eminence."

"You will drive me tomorrow, Tomas. I want you to plan our route so that we will arrive shortly before the high mass begins at noon."

"Yes, Your Eminence."

"Now, if you will leave me, all of you. I would like to be alone."

When he heard the doors close he went into the bedroom. Bashar jumped up on him and, wrestling with the big dog, he knelt on the floor for several minutes of rough play. Later, he went to the window and looked out at the lights of the city, at the dark vein of river circling among those lights. Bashar barked and, turning, he saw Kris coming through the study. "I found it, Eminence."

He took the sheets of corrected typescript and sat on the worn leather sofa, reading rapidly. "Kris? Listen to this."

He read aloud. " 'On the floor of this forest are millions of pine needles. It takes only a spark to set them ablaze. And what is that spark? Is it not the recent proof that those who rule us hold the Church in the utmost contempt? This callous behavior toward the religious leadership of the nation could be the spark,' et cetera. . . . *What* recent proof is he talking about?"

Kris stared at him, puzzled.

"This speech was written for delivery tomorrow, but it was written before the Christian Fighters kidnapped me. Therefore Krasnoy knew that they were going to kidnap me. Later, I would believe that it was the Security Police who had kidnapped me. This demonstration would have taken place, and all the time I would have been innocent of what was really going on."

"But, Eminence? If the Christian Fighters tried to get you out of the way before, they might well try again tomorrow."

"I don't think so. The man who tried to kill me wasn't part of Keller's plan. Besides, it won't be so easy now. You forget that the Security Police have appointed themselves as my official bodyguards."

"Is there anything I can get for you, anything I can do for you tonight, Eminence?"

"Yes, Kris. Pray."

22

Rain clouds bursting from the gray morning sky
sent sheets of summer rain skimming along the surface of the highway as his car rushed toward the
outskirts of Gneisk. Ahead, two SP Ladas raced up
to intersections, checking that the route ahead was
clear. Behind his car two other blue Ladas filled
with armed plainclothesmen followed closely. Before leaving the capital he had informed the SP of
his destination and now they guarded and guided
his car as though they were an official escort. In the
suburbs of the city of Gneisk their progress slowed
as they began to encounter the tail end of pilgrimage
traffic, buses with extra passengers sitting on the
roofs, motorcars loaded beyond capacity and, as they
left the city going in the direction of Jasna mountain, farm trucks and farm carts filled with peasant
families, the carts' drivers standing up behind the
shafts, whipping on the horses for fear of arriving
late.

Now, on the road, paper papal flags began to be
seen at those small roadside shrines to the Virgin,
which had survived forty years of Communist rule.
Ahead was the mountain's bulk and the spire of the
church at Rywald. His car, its passageway cleared
by the police, was recognized. A cheer went up and
the people in other cars bowed in respect as he waved
in a gesture of blessing. "There are more pilgrims

than ever," Kris said, peering out of the car window.

"Is it religion or is it politics?" he asked. "Do they come here to worship God, or to defy the government?"

"To worship, surely, Eminence. I believe the people's faith is stronger now than at any time in our history."

"Do you really believe that, Kris?"

He felt his secretary's discomfort. After a moment, Kris said, "What do you mean, Eminence?"

"I think our people are using religion now as a sort of politics. To remind themselves that we are a Catholic nation while our enemies are not. To remind us that we always continued to be a nation even when the name of our country was taken off the map. It's all part of our collective memory and we cherish it. But what has it got to do with our love of God?"

"Perhaps it's brought us closer to God, Eminence?"

"I wonder. Are we filling the churches because we love God more than before? Or do we do it out of nostalgia for the past, or, worse, to defy the government? Because if we do, Kris, then God is mocked."

The police cars began to honk again as they came to a place where cars had been parked on both sides of a narrow road, and their occupants joined hundreds of worshipers, now proceeding on foot toward the lower slopes of the mountain, beginning to climb the worn footpaths past ugly stone stations of the cross. The one narrow road that led up the mountain to the Rywald Shrine was closed off by wooden traffic barriers. Two priests, recognizing him, opened the barriers, respectfully waving them on.

The police cars preceded him along the now empty road, leaving behind floods of hawkers, who held up cheap plastic statuettes, pearl rosaries and painted banners proclaiming the anniversary of the Blessed Martyrs. After a few hundred yards the road came to an end. Ahead, in the cobblestoned square below the church, he saw some thirty parked vehicles, the cars of priests and officials who were already in the church preparing for the services. As they drove into the square, half a dozen men and women hurried toward their car, some with cameras, some with microphones and sound equipment. "No interviews," he said to Kris. "No comment." He leaned over and pointed a route to Tomas. "Drive on through. We will park above the square, directly behind the sacristy."

Avoiding the press, their car went up a narrow alley that led to the rear of the church. The SP men, confused, restarted their engines and followed. At the rear entrance Bishop Cihon, secretary of the Gneisk commemoration committee, was waiting.

"Good morning, Your Eminence. Welcome to Rywald."

Cihon, a tall stately person, was already robed for the ceremonies. As he came forward in welcome he glanced nervously at the SP men who jumped out of their cars and at once formed a ring around the side door of the church, glancing suspiciously this way and that. "Is something wrong?" Cihon asked, nervously.

"No, no," he said. "These gentlemen are here to protect me."

One of the SP men detached himself from the others and came over to him. "Excuse me, Your Eminence, but it would help us if we knew where you are going to sit at the ceremony and what you are going to do in the next half hour." The SP man looked at his watch. "The mass starts at noon, is that correct, sir?"

"At noon, yes," he said. "And, in the meantime, I wish to be alone. I will go to the sacristy now and change for the ceremony. I will remain in the sacristy, at prayer, until mass is about to begin. Then I will come into the church as part of the procession and sit in my chair at the right-hand side of the main altar. You will see the chair and its position if you go into the church. At the end of the ceremony I will go to the rostrum and deliver a short address, which will be broadcast by loudspeakers to those who are on the mountainside. When I have finished speaking I will go down to the altar rails and give communion. This will be the start of the communion services that will be given by priests to the pilgrims on the mountain slopes. And then?" He turned to Cihon.

"After the services we will drive to Archbishop Krasnoy's residence for lunch," Cihon said.

"Thank you, Your Eminence," the SP man said. "May I put four of my men on the altar? I assure you they will keep out of sight."

He looked at Cihon. "What do you think?"

"I don't know what this is all about," Cihon said. "Who would harm you, Your Eminence?"

The SP man ignored this and said to him, "Please sir, I am responsible to General Vrona for your safety. If you will please help us?"

"Very well," he said. "But they must not be seen by the congregation. Kris, what time is it?"

"Eleven-thirty-five, Eminence."

"Let us go into the sacristy, then. I would like to go over my sermon before I change. Tomas, will you bring my things?"

"Archbishop Krasnoy sends his apologies," Cihon said. They went into the church and along a rear corridor leading to the sacristy. "It seems there was some last-minute problem with the loudspeakers and he's gone down into Gneisk to speak with the electricians. He will join us just before the ceremonies begin."

"Shall I go in with you, Eminence?" Kris Malik asked when they reached the sacristy door.

"No, that won't be necessary. Just check with those SP men as to where they are to be stationed. They mustn't be seen."

"Yes, Eminence."

Tomas, carrying a heavy suitcase, opened the sacristy door, and waited for him to enter.

"I will leave you here, Eminence," Cihon said. "If you will excuse me, I have to speak with the choir."

"Of course."

When he entered the sacristy he was surprised not to see more priests inside. Usually at times like this there was a certain crowding and confusion as various arriving clerics used the sacristy to change for the ceremony. But only two priests were in the sacristy, one wearing blue-and-gold vestments and a second priest dressed in a long white surplice, who was trying to fix a silver censer that seemed to be broken. Both bowed respectfully and the priest in vestments said, "Good morning, Your Eminence. If you will come this way, we have a room here where you can change and rest until the ceremonies begin."

The priest in vestments then led him through the sacristy and into a little room just off it. It was furnished with pine cupboards in which altar clothes and vestments were stored. Nearby, on a long table, were laid out silver patens for the communion. There was a high-backed pine chair and, in a corner, a prie-dieu. The priest in vestments, smiling and bowing, left him alone in this room with Tomas, who at once opened the suitcase, and, clearing a place on the long table, began to lay out his crimson robes.

He looked up at the small window. It was barred and a stream of sunlight fell like a holy light on the worn pine cupboards in which the vestments were stored. He opened his briefcase and took out the few handwritten pages he had prepared last night. He placed them on the ledge of one of the cupboards, arranging them in order and uncapping his old Waterman fountain pen. As he did, he heard the door open behind him and two priests, wearing long white linen surplices with black skirted cassocks underneath, entered the room, closing the door behind them.

"Good morning, Your Eminence," the first priest said. Sparse blond hair rose like an aureole around the back of his pink skull. He smiled and bobbed his head respectfully. The other priest was young, with a wispy red beard. He was Prisbek. The first "priest," pulling up his white surplice, took a revolver from the deep pocket of his cassock and waved it at Tomas. It was the revolver, rather than his face, that made him remember this "priest." It was the same revolver that had been pointed at him three days ago at the Ricany checkpoint.

"Put that away, Colonel," he said. "There is no need for it."

The pink-faced man shrugged. "Actually, Colonel Poulnikov was a nom de guerre," he said. "And you were quite right, Eminence. Poulnikov *is* a Russian name. Actually, my real name is of German origin. Keller. Waldemar Keller. I believe you knew my uncle. He was a member of the government-in-exile, in London, during the war."

"I remember his name," he said. "But I was fifteen years old then and living here. Is he still alive?"

"He died five years ago," Keller said. "But I hope that his ideals live on."

"Indeed," he said. "And do you think your uncle would have tried to murder a cardinal of the Catholic Church?"

"We did not try to murder you!" Keller said, a flush rising from his cheeks to his pink-skinned forehead. "The person who tried to kill you was going directly against my orders. He was a maniac. It has never been our intention to harm you."

"But it was your intention to kidnap me and hold me while you plotted with Archbishop Krasnoy to bring this country to a state of civil insurrection. Would your uncle have approved of terrorist tactics—blowing up innocent young men while they were asleep?"

"What are you talking about?" Keller said, angrily. "What young men?"

"The young soldiers you tried to kill two nights ago in Praha barracks."

"They are government soldiers," Keller said. "The barracks was a military target. What do you think those soldiers are used for, if not to keep us under Communist rule?"

"Military targets?" he said. "I did not know we were at war. Those are our soldiers—eighteen-year-old conscripts, most of them—your countrymen and mine. And who are you, who is anyone, to decide that we must enter another decade of violence, arrests, imprisonments and deaths? You promised Bishop Charnowski and poor Krasnoy, for all I know, that there would be no violence. But you *want* violence, don't you, Keller? You are using the Church as a dupe. And I do not intend to let that happen."

"If you will pardon my saying so, Eminence, the matter is now out of your hands. You will not attend the ceremonies this morning. Unfortunately, you will be taken ill. We shall have to send for an ambulance and bring you to the hospital in Gneisk, where you will be kept in intensive care for a few days. When you have recovered you will be released. You can then make any statement you wish. I hope, by that time, you will be seen for what you truly are, a careerist, and a collaborator with this godless regime."

He turned away from Keller and looked at Tomas, who stood, holding a crimson sash, staring at the intruders. "Tomas," he said. "I am going to get dressed now."

Keller laughed. "Why do you want to get dressed? You are going to hospital, not to mass." He raised the revolver, pointing. "Sit down."

He ignored this and began to remove his clothes. "I said sit down!" Keller said.

"Why should I? Are you going to shoot me? If I am found shot it will not suit your plans at all. After my broadcast last night I doubt that anyone would believe that I was shot by the SP."

"Father Prisbek," Keller said. "Please?"

He saw Prisbek cross the room and go to a small sink beside the vestments cupboard. "All right, Tomas," he said. "Help me with this sash." He stepped into the scarlet cassock and buttoned it up as Tomas began to wind the sash around his waist. He saw Keller sit on the long table, dangling his leg.

"You're extraordinarily arrogant, aren't you?" Keller said. "Still, I suppose it will add a touch of *verismo* if you are wearing your ceremonial robes. Taken ill, while robing for the ceremony. Why not? Prisbek?"

Prisbek, bending over the sink, said, "Just a moment. The suction is—"

"Hurry!" Keller said. He stood up and pointed his revolver at Tomas. "Come here," he said. "Kneel down."

At that moment, Prisbek turned from the sink, holding up a syringe. Tomas advanced uncertainly toward Keller. "Kneel here," Keller ordered. Tomas, fearful, looked up. "Your Eminence?"

"Tomas, don't!" he said, suddenly. As he did, Keller looked at him, then stepped forward and clubbed Tomas at the base of his skull. Tomas fell on the floor.

He knew what he must do. He ran to the door, which was not locked. He opened it and, with Prisbek at his heels, ran through the sacristy and out into the corridor. He heard them behind him, gaining on him. At that moment he turned a corner in the corridor and opened a door that led into the church itself.

The church was packed. As he came through the door he almost stumbled on people who knelt in the side aisle. Music, loud and triumphant, sounded from the organ in the loft above him. The worshipers, surprised, turned to look at his robed, scarlet figure. People bowed reverently, making way for him in the crowded aisle.

Keller and Prisbek, in their white surplices, their faces naked with anxiety, hurried up behind him. "You are not well, Your Eminence," Keller said, softly. Reaching out, Keller took hold of his arm, then turned to Prisbek, who held up the syringe.

"Your injection, Eminence," Prisbek said.

In the packed pews on either side of the aisle people sat, staring. Keller was holding his arm, scrabbling to pull up the sleeve of his robe. In the struggle, which became an undignified scuffle, he managed to knock the syringe out of Prisbek's hand. "Let go of me!" he said, but a surge of triumphal music drowned his voice. Now three ushers were hurrying up the aisle.

"What's wrong? Is His Eminence all right?"

He looked at Keller's flushed face, then signaled to the ushers. "I will take my seat now," he said. He saw Keller draw back, saw Prisbek stoop and pick up the syringe. "Come," he said to the ushers, and accompanied by them, went up the side aisle into the main aisle of the nave, walking quickly and purposefully toward the altar. At the right of the altar was a high-backed bishop's chair. People in the crowded pews and balconies peered at him, puzzled that he should appear before the official procession. He opened the gate of the communion rail and went up the steps, genuflecting to the altar. Then he sat in the ceremonial chair and looked out at the congregation. Sweat ran in trickles down his brow, stinging his eyes. He bowed his head. At that moment, the music stopped and, high above in the choir loft, a pure soprano voice began to sing the "Ave Maria."

He looked behind him. There, stationed discreetly behind the choir stalls, was a plainclothes SP man, and another, also out of sight of the congregation, squatted down behind the altar. As he turned back to face the congregation, Kris Malik, genuflecting to the altar, came up the steps and bent toward him.

"Eminence, are you all right?"

"Yes. Are the ceremonies about to begin?"

"The procession is forming. Bishop Wior will celebrate the mass, assisted by Bishop Cihon and Father Pruss. Archbishop Krasnoy will give the address after the general communion."

As he delivered this information, Kris looked at him, waiting for him to object.

"Tell them to proceed, then," he said.

"Very good, Eminence." Kris, surprised, went back down the altar steps and through the sacristy door.

He looked up at the clock at the rear of the church. It was six minutes to twelve. He was aware that the congregation was eyeing him with surprise and that people were leaning toward each other to whisper. Suddenly, the high, pure soprano voice in the choir was erased by a harsh clatter in the skies above the church, a noise that he recognized as the sound of helicopters coming in to land. The noise became deafening, then slowly subsided. Again, the congregation shifted, peering about. The main doors at the rear of the church were opened and about twenty uniformed police and SP men came in, in a phalanx, pushing their way through the worshipers who were kneeling in the center aisle. The police were followed by a group of men and women he recognized as the foreign-press contingent he had seen earlier, in the courtyard. All moved toward the two rows of benches roped off directly below the communion rail. There was a scuffling and a blinking of flashbulbs as the whole congregation swiveled around in their seats in a movement of surprise.

For a moment he was not sure what was happening. Then, as the photographers backed toward the altar, he saw, moving up the main aisle, wearing the gray-green general's uniform that was his political trademark, the Prime Minister, General Urban. Behind Urban, uneasy, as though he walked in an enemy minefield, was the small obsequiously sinister figure of Vrona, in dark suit and tie, his shirt dazzlingly white, his hair slicked flat on his skull.

The Prime Minister came to the roped-off benches. He did not look around or genuflect to the altar, but took his seat directly in the center of the row. SP men at once sat on either side of him. Vrona took a seat in the row directly behind him, while the foreign press scrambled to occupy the remaining vacant places. At that moment the organ pealed. Through a side door the procession of bishops and priests began to file onto the altar, the bishops taking their places in a row of choir stalls. The three priests who would act as celebrants of the mass moved to the center of the altar, genuflecting. One of them, Bishop Wior, turned then and bowed to him.

At that he knelt on the prie-dieu beside his chair. The mass began. The church seemed electric with tension and curiosity. That General Urban, Prime Minister of a Marxist government, should attend a Catholic mass was an event without precedent. Heads turned to see if he had knelt down, but he had not. He sat, his arms folded across his chest, staring at the proceedings as though he were a presiding judge.

In the choir stalls, the first pew was occupied by Archbishop Krasnoy, his florid features emphasized by the white-and-gold vestments he wore. He saw Krasnoy eye the General, then scan the church and the throng of worshipers. The other bishops, similarly distracted from their prayers, had about them a vague air of alarm and uncertainty, as though they already knew what Krasnoy planned to say in his address and now, face-to-face with the enemy, feared what would happen. Only John Charnowski, his head shaking from his illness, bent forward, eyes closed, lost in urgent prayer.

The great mass of people in the seats and aisles shuffled like some huge animal as they knelt and stood. In the gloom of the church, the altar glowed bright with candles and floodlights: shafts of sunlight striking down through the multicolored stained-glass windows as, high in the choir loft, voices sang the *kyrie eleison*. The sound was carried out through powerful loudspeakers to the mountainside, where thousands of worshipers knelt in the open air. He thought of the helicopters landing in the courtyard below the church, seen by those thousands of people, and knew that, like an earthquake's tremor, the fact of this encounter was now spreading across the land. Why has Urban come here? What has he heard? Does he think that his presence will intimidate Krasnoy and forestall the demonstration? What is in his mind?

He looked down from his prie-dieu into the Prime Minister's face. The mass was approaching that sacred moment when bread and wine would be changed into the body and blood of Jesus Christ. He watched the Prime Minister as the little consecration bell was rung, its faint tinkle carried by loudspeakers out to the crowds beyond the walls of the church. Then, as the priest raised the Host for all to adore, he saw the Prime Minister flinch at this reminder of his past and, in an involuntary gesture of reverence, briefly bow his head. Looking down at Francis Urban's bowed head, he thought of the boy he had known in school, and remembering that boy, now a balding man in a general's uniform, prayed to God to save Francis Urban's immortal soul. And as he prayed he saw the Prime Minister raise his head and look at him, as though, by some telepathy, he had guessed the content of his prayer. The consecration bell rang a second time. The priest raised the silver chalice in which wine had become Christ's blood. All of the congregation bowed, save Vrona and the SP men who watched as though, at any moment, shooting might break out. The consecration bell rang again. The mass continued.

Now, in the bishops' pews, he saw heads turn and whispering begin as the moment of communion approached. On the main altar the celebrant ate the wafer of bread and drank the wine that had been changed into the body and blood of Christ. In a few minutes, scores, perhaps hundreds, of people would receive communion. He saw Krasnoy rise and come from the bishops' pews, as though to make an announcement directing the communicants to come forward. But, as Krasnoy made his way toward the rostrum, he carried a thick sheaf of notes in his hand. This was no announcement. Krasnoy had decided to outwit him.

He rose, quickly, from his cardinal's chair. He walked down toward the rostrum, which was directly beneath him. Krasnoy, who had to cross the altar to reach the rostrum, was caught midway and hesitated.

In that crucial moment, having reached the rostrum, he put his hand over the microphone, claiming it, then, turning, looked at his adversary. Krasnoy's blood-filled face darkened as though he would suffer a stroke. He stood at mid-altar, twisting the sheaf of notes in his hands, then, turning unsteadily as though he were drunk or ill, he walked back to his seat.

He waited until Krasnoy was seated, then, gripping the sides of the rostrum, stared out into the waiting silence of the church. At the side door he saw that Keller and Prisbek were standing by the wall, waiting, listening. But he no longer feared them. I have reached this place at last. God give me the words I need.

"Beloved," he said. "I am addressing you now, before the mass is ended, because it is my hope that when you have taken Holy Communion you will, for a moment, pray, and reflect upon my words. We are assembled at this holy shrine in remembrance of one hundred and ten men and women massacred on this spot because of their faith, two hundred years ago, this day. Their fate has entered our history. It is a reminder that there are times when resistance, violence, even death, are preferable to tyranny. Two hundred years have passed and we still live under tyranny: the tyranny of an age when religious beliefs have become inextricably entwined with political hatreds, when, day after day, in countries all around us, innocent people die from bombings, from terrorist attacks, from political and religious reprisals and revenge. I am an inadequate leader. I have allowed my people to come to the brink of such violence, to a confusion between the wrongs that have been done to us and the wrongs that some among us now advocate that we do in return. I beg you to think of the deaths of others. Remember, the terrorist and the tyrant have that in common. They do not think of those deaths. I tell you now. There must be no demonstration of the national will, no demonstration of any kind. Remember that, no matter which government rules us, we remain a free people, free in our minds, free in an unfree state. That is the greater heroism that is called for on this day, so pregnant with events, and so filled with anxieties. I beg you. Go in peace."

He bowed his head, then raised his right hand in signal to the choir. As the organ pealed out the first bars of the national hymn, the congregation rose to its feet. He looked down at the faces beneath him and sensed in the fervor of voices that God had granted his wish. General Urban and General Vrona had risen with the others and stood, not singing, but staring straight ahead. He looked back at Archbishop Krasnoy, who met his eye, then bowed his head as in a gesture of submission.

The hymn was ending. Voices rose in clamor to the vaulted roofs, voices that carried out to the mountainside, where thousands of worshipers took up the refrain, the voices ebbing, lost in the winds. God has taken me through these days. He has given me the strength to do His will.

He looked across the church to where Keller and Prisbek stood. Surprised, he saw that both were singing the anthem. The words of St. Paul came again into his mind: *How unsearchable are His judgments, how inscrutable His ways.*

The music ceased. He signaled to one of the attendant priests. He stepped down from the rostrum and, taking a chalice from the waiting priest, he led the procession toward the communion rail.

He lifted a Host from the chalice, holding it up for all to see. Then, as the first communicants came forward to kneel at the railing, he stepped down to meet them. Joy filled him. At last, he knew peace. He placed the small circle of unleavened Host on the tongue of a young woman. Accepting it, she closed her eyes in reverence. He raised another Host from the silver chalice.

But the next communicant did not open her mouth. She stared up at him, her eyes dilating as in fear, and he saw on her bruised cheeks the small cuts made by broken glass four nights ago in Proclamation Square. Then he saw the revolver that she had taken from her handbag and in that moment knew: This is God's will. Yet, as Danekin's sister, trembling, raised the gun, pointing it at his chest, he felt a moment's hesitation. It was as though he stood on the edge of a dark crevasse, unable to see to the other side. The silence of God: would it change at the moment of his death? He held up the Host as though to give it to her. He saw her finger tighten on the trigger.

And heard that terrible noise.